OCD, The DUDE, and ME

a novel by
LAUREN ROEDY VAUGHN

DIAL BOOKS
an imprint of Penguin Group (USA) inc.

DIAL BOOKS

An imprint of Penguin Group (USA) Inc.

Published by The Penguin Group

Penguin Group (USA) Inc., 375 Hudson Street, New York, NY 10014, U.S.A. • Penguin Group (Canada), 90 Eglinton Avenue East, Suite 700, Toronto, Ontario, Canada M4P 2Y3 (a division of Pearson Penguin Canada Inc.) • Penguin Books Ltd, 80 Strand, London WC2R 0RL, England • Penguin Ireland, 25 St. Stephen's Green, Dublin 2, Ireland (a division of Penguin Books Ltd) • Penguin Group (Australia), 707 Collins Street, Melbourne, Victoria 3008, Australia (a division of Pearson Australia Group Pty Ltd) • Penguin Books India Pvt Ltd, 11 Community Centre, Panchsheel Park, New Delhi - 110 017, India • Penguin Group (NZ), 67 Apollo Drive, Rosedale, Auckland 0632, New Zealand (a division of Pearson New Zealand Ltd) • Penguin Books (South Africa), Rosebank Office Park, 181 Jan Smuts Avenue, Parktown North 2193, South Africa • Penguin China, B7 Jiaming Center, 27 East Third Ring Road North, Chaoyang District, Beijing 100020, China • Penguin Books Ltd, Registered Offices: 80 Strand, London WC2R 0RL, England

10 9 8 7 6 5 4 3 2 1

Library of Congress Cataloging-in-Publication Data

Vaughn, Lauren Roedy.
    OCD, the dude, and me / Lauren Roedy Vaughn.
        p. cm.
    Summary: Danielle Levine stands out even at her alternative high school—in appearance and attitude—but when her scathing and sometimes raunchy English essays land her in a social skills class, she meets Daniel, another social misfit who may break her resolve to keep everyone at arm's length.
    ISBN 978-0-8037-3843-0 (hardback)
    [1. Interpersonal relations—Fiction. 2. High schools—Fiction. 3. Schools—Fiction. 4. Obsessive-compulsive disorder—Fiction. 5. Emotional problems—Fiction.] I. Title.
    PZ7.V466Ocd 2013
    [Fic]—dc23
                                                    2012025357

"The world is not respectable; it is mortal, tormented, confused, deluded forever; but it is shot through with beauty, with love, with glints of courage and laughter; and in these, the spirit blooms . . ."
—*George Santayana*

SENIOR YEAR WRITINGS

Organized and compiled by
Danielle Carmen Levine

I should be getting ready for school right now, but I'm not because my mother has thrown off the flow of the morning. When she came in my room to bring me my new Adderall prescription, she tripped on the Romantic Era section of my library, books which are alphabetized, systematized, and laid out on the floor. It took all summer for me to get them exactly where I want them. It makes me happy just to look at them. When she tripped, she scattered the stacks out of order. I don't think it took longer than five seconds before my body started shaking. I crunched myself into a fetal position and started to breathe as deeply as possible. Mom told me to calm down, like it's no big deal to rebuild perfection. Austen's works are now mixed with the Brontë sisters. I can't find Browning. Wordsworth is under my bed, and Blake and Shelley have been kicked to a pile of dirty clothes near my dresser. I don't have time to realphabetize them, and Mom is starting to lose her patience, pointing out I could choose to use my time doing that, instead of sitting here and typing out my angst. She's wrong. Typing out my angst is *exactly* what I need to do if I'm going to get myself in any functional state for school. After all she says "It's not a library" but rather a cluster of books I keep on the floor for people to trip over. According to her "libraries have shelves." I told her shelves are not included in the technical definition of "library." She told me to quit it with the semantics and get dressed. Whatever.

Another huge issue is that I wanted to finish gluing the pieces of charming postcards I cut up to decorate this year's "me-moir" binder, my fourth writing collection. Each year's binder—the sacred place I keep all my school essays, journals, personal me-moir entries, e-mails, etc. My writing is best served contained, away from the eyes of others, but that doesn't mean it shouldn't have exquisite packaging. Obviously.

Since freshman year when my parents forced me to go to a "special school," these binders are the only things that have made it bearable. Intense planning and a sea of supplies are required to build the perfect home for chronicling my life. It's the best living history I've got. Every entry has its own color-coded sheet protector. Last week, I cut up six postcards, all with scenes of loving couplehood from the nineteenth century that weren't a fit among the crowd taped on my headboard. Once it's finished, they will fit together like an ornate puzzle. Which. Is. Awesome. Or would be, if this weren't the first day of senior year and hundreds of pieces remain unglued.

At least my back-to-school outfit is staying the same. There is no question about that. I am wearing my black combat Chucks and have managed to untangle my XL burgundy T-shirt from the twisted pile on my bed, which is where my tees like to live. My black leggings and black beret with the tiny feather that stands straight up will complete my look of "rotted lonely pear in bowl"—a still life. Appropriate.

4

CLASS ASSIGNMENT 9/10
Essay #1: My Biography

(This is what I turned in and got a C+ on after having to read it in front of the class because Ms. Harrison believes in "publishing" as an important part of the writing process. Make no mistake: I did not read the introduction or the conclusion aloud. Also, I have no interest in Ms. Harrison's humiliating version of "publishing." Clearly, I've got my own system for that.)

Danielle Levine

English 12

Ms. Harrison

Period 4

Ms. Harrison, I liked the authors' tea you planned where we all discussed the books we chose to read over the summer. I hope you could tell by my class comments that I liked *Wuthering Heights*. You have no idea how much my parents got in to reading that book with me. And, well, I got in to it, too. I dressed as Catherine. I have a lot of vintage dresses with puffy sleeves and petticoats (which generally stay in my closet) and a bunch of hats, from every era imaginable, and those were appropriate accents for this family read-aloud. (Very important note: don't tell any of my classmates that we dressed up and read the book together. Please.) While my parents may have fantasized that their love lives were akin to Catherine and Heathcliff's, let me assure you that the truth is no such thing. They were raised in the lap of luxury; they fell in love in college and have stayed in love; and they both make tons of money. Their hearts have never been torn asunder. I think this is a good place to transition into the meat of the essay you are looking for.

I am adopted. My parents' names are Doug and Evelyn. I don't mind being adopted. I have no idea who my biological parents are. Most people know immediately that I am adopted because I don't look anything like my parents. (Neither of them has a wild nest of red hair or thunder thighs.) My dad is a doctor and my mom is a successful real estate agent. I think about how she is a *real, estate* agent because she sells big houses to rich people. I could never be a real estate agent because once my clients saw that I had to lock every outside door at least fifty times after a tour, they'd never call me again. LOL, but it's true. And, a doctor? No way. No one's life should be left in my hands. I can barely do math; I couldn't possibly tackle problems related to the human body. Makes me dizzy just *contemplating* it. (Btw, Ms. Harrison, if you want our essays to include the vocabulary words you are teaching us, you are going to have to allow me to italicize them. I cannot just let a new word blend in with my old vocabulary. Thank you.)

I've attended Meadow Oaks School since the ninth grade. This school (as you know) is for high-potential students with learning disabilities, which is a *euphemistic* phrase for kids who don't do well in school in some areas but whose IQs are still fine somehow. We're all smart, but we have various "academic issues" that require some specific help from experts. You know the deal. What I like best about this school is that since almost everyone is Jewish, we get off a lot because of religious holidays. My family is no religion, so I don't have to go to temple or church on the holidays. Usually on those days I read.

I don't have any brothers and sisters or any pets. I have a housekeeper, Martha, and I'm very grateful for her because of my "materials management problems" as you call it. "Materials management" sounds more like a major in business college than a personal problem. You can just say I'm messy. I won't be offended; I'm not blind to the truth. My own mother tells me my backpack "looks like a cyclone hit it."

My mom recently redecorated our two-story house to "reflect her aesthetic" of warm-colored walls and brightly colored accent pieces, but she left my room alone because clutter, scratches on the hardwood floors, and hats hanging on the wall are my aesthetic. People who love garage sales or go antiquing would love my room. But, don't misunderstand, nothing in there is for sale.

My parents bought me a used hybrid vehicle so I can drive myself to school in a responsible way, but I have to pay my own car insurance. I get paid to walk the neighbors' dogs up in the hills where we live, south of the boulevard in the Valley, and that is how I have money to pay for my phone and fund my snow globe obsession. Generally, I get snow globes whenever I go on trips, and I like the ones that have scenic or gentle images that are frozen in time. I don't know why. I just do.

Teacher comments: *If you have aside comments, please make an appointment to speak with me. Include only ideas relevant to the topic.*

QUICK JOURNAL #2 9/10
Just talking myself down

Writing "my biography" essay at the start of senior year sent me into somewhat of a tailspin. I survived the first days of school by wearing the right shoes and hats and by avoiding any vulnerable contact with the pretty and popular crowd (Heather, Sara, James, John, etc.), who make being at school look so easy. But once I had to start writing about myself (even though I like doing that under the right circumstances), I suffered a case of vertigo. I had to lie on my bed under my T-shirts for a bit.

Here is my current loop of obsessive thoughts: 1. It bothers me to think about all the upcoming school events that I will be alone for. 2. Just like every other year, I hate that Heather cuts in front of me in the lunch line and whips out her phone and starts talking so I can't say anything. 3. I keep thinking about that day in PE last year, where I was the only person who couldn't run the mile without taking breaks. My classmates, possessed of personal trainers, low heart rates, and taut physiques finished the run in like two seconds. By the second lap, I was gasping for air and so sweaty that they probably took bets on whether or not I'd die of a heart attack right before their eyes. I had hoped I would.

I have reordered the snow globes on my dresser about a hundred times. They are very calming. Nearly all of them depict life's perfect moments, and when I give myself time to stare at them, they offer hope of a better world. Now they are in proper clusters. Farmhouses, landscapes, and historic monuments on the left, playful girls in the center, and couples in love on the right.

Next I'm going to try on all my hats and then stare at the postcards on my headboard to lose myself in a fantasy, where I convince myself that someday I will be somewhere other than right here.

(I love this essay even though Ms. Harrison did not because it was not organized and the tone was too informal, which Ms. Harrison is obsessed with. B- from Ms. Harrison but A+ from my aunt Joyce who read the essay and loved it.)

Danielle Levine

English 12

Ms. Harrison

Period 4

It was really wonderful to think about something wonderful. The sun was coming in through my bedroom window as I sat at my desk to write, so I put on my bright yellow Chucks and yellow sunhat and tried to let their happy color and the sun's warmth sink into me in order to come up with a good topic. It worked! I have decided to write this essay about my aunt Joyce.

My aunt Joyce is forty-two years old, single, and has no kids. Now, before you get any prejudicial ideas about what she is like, let me tell you. My aunt Joyce is spectacular. She is beautiful: blond hair, thin thighs, smooth voice, perfect finger-nails, great clothes—which she looks great in because she is a size two and a fashion designer. She gets me the most amazing hats and cool clothes, reflecting a time before sewing machines (lots of ribbons and laces), that we pull out of my closet and try on when we're together. My mom has very short brown hair that highlights her bone structure but which does not lend itself to petticoats and flowery bonnets; however, sometimes she joins us for our costume parties anyway. Like the time we all tied ourselves into these elaborate corsets and pretended we lived the lives of the women I only read about. So fun. (However, I do worry those women were never able to take a deep breath while dressed. Terrible.) Besides classic and stylish clothing, Joyce has turned me on to some old music like Tom Petty, and I've turned her on to The Romantic Era, which is an awesome band (all six of the guys are so cute it's unbelievable; you should check out their album. They have one song about Juliet . . . as in *Romeo and* . . . I think it's right up your alley).

My aunt Joyce is not what your mind might jump to when you think single white female. Anyway, she and a friend did this WONDERFUL thing. They threw a shower for themselves! It was tight.

My aunt Joyce told me that over the course of her life she went to so many baby showers and wedding showers that she couldn't keep track of them all. So one day, she and her friend Karen were talking about all the time, attention, and money they spent on going to their girlfriends' showers and how that time, attention, and money was probably never going to be *reciprocated* because they were destined to be single and child-less for the rest of their lives, and while that is a fine thing to be, they would never have the fun of registering for gifts and having people celebrate them in a way that was not about their age. So they decided to "f*** social constraints" as my aunt put it and throw themselves a shower. (Isn't that wonderful? I mean, really.)

They both registered at Pottery Barn and Target. (Joyce told me that at Target they asked all kinds of questions about her registry, and she was forced to make it a bridal registry, and so she had to make up the name of her fiancé, and she gave the name of a super-famous movie star that she has had a mad crush on forever, but I won't out that here because Aunt Joyce's decade-long fantasy crush is her business, and she played all *coy* when the salesgirl asked if it "was the real so-and-so" and the salesgirl got all excited because my aunt wouldn't deny the *veracity* of the claim, but how silly, because why would a movie star's wife-to-be register at Target? Please.)

Anyway, the party was at my house, and the women in my family love a good garden party. My aunt put my hair up in a Gibson girl–style, and, for a change, I felt very sophisticated out in actual life. Mom bought out every florist shop in Los Angeles to decorate, and she ordered three large ice sculptures for the backyard. Stunning. The hummingbirds my mom knows and loves (she actually names them) were out in full force, and they were the background music of the day. We had afternoon tea, played charades and croquet, and watched Joyce and Karen open presents in the backyard garden of my house. Just writing about the day makes me feel light as air. (That feeling rarely happens to me.)

I may be single my whole life, but my aunt will help me cope with whatever I become. Aunt Joyce and her shower are wonderful!

Teacher comments: *Don't use profanity—ever—in these essays. You are lucky to have Aunt Joyce.*

✶ CLASS ASSIGNMENT ✶ 10/5
Essay #3: Free Write

(What I, of course, do not turn in, and in fact, plan to hide immediately in my me-moir binder, lock checked multiple times.)

Danielle Levine

English 12

Ms. Harrison

Period 4

A "free-write essay" this early in the year? Really? Giving a free-write essay is a total cop-out for a teacher. Ms. Harrison has a poster on her wall that says, "Always give your best effort." Apparently, her posters don't apply to her. Very irritating. But I'm even more irritated that she made us write down on a piece of paper the name of one person who we would like to room with on the school trip to England. I wanted to write "FU" in really big letters on my slip and see if she got the point. Then I wanted to write "Jacob Kingston," which is the truth, but if I wrote it instead of just thinking it, I'm sure Ms. Harrison would refer me to the school psychologist and then call my parents because I didn't have the good sense to know that I couldn't room with a boy. And then I'd want to scream: I'M BEING *FACETIOUS*, YOU IDIOTS. DON'T YOU GET IT?! NEVER IN MY LIFE WILL I EVER SLEEP WITH A BOY LIKE JACOB KINGSTON. I just spilled my soda all over my already messy but expensive antique desk! (I hid under a pile of fresh laundry for a minute to prevent a panic attack, which I did, good job. I've emerged and can write again.)

Instead, I just wrote on the slip: *no one will want to room with me.* And then I know I sound like a whiny victim, but it is true. Any name I might write on that slip of paper will be *tantamount* to disappointment. I am *anathema* to everyone in my class. On the drive home up into the hills of my landscaped neighborhood, I thought about how messy this whole situation is, and I had a big talk with myself, out loud, about how bad this trip is for me. There is no way I can conceive of doing all the things I like to do on trips to England while I'm with the kids in my class. I will be taunted right off the planet if I ask for a moment to go get a snow globe or some sepia-toned postcards or spout Shakespeare aloud while strolling through Stratford-upon-Avon dressed as Ophelia. OMG, but I'm starting to hyperventilate just writing that.

When I got home and told my parents that I absolutely don't want to go on this trip, they said I have to, especially since they told the school that they would pay for a student who couldn't afford to go. I told them to save the money and just pay for the other person and not me. No dice, they say. They want me to socialize, not have my head in a book the entire time. No one is going to want to room with me, Mom. Nonsense, she says in her everything-is-always-glorious way. She's so clueless sometimes. During dinner, I wore my blue ski mask over my face in protest. Dad insisted I take it off because I was disrespecting my mother. I didn't. I had to eat dinner in my room. Fine.

CLASS ASSIGNMENT 10/7
Essay #4: The Class Trip

(How I really felt but did not turn in for fear that I would have to read it in front of the class. I did not make an appointment to tell Ms. Harrison my thoughts. These are my thoughts, just for me.)

Danielle Levine
English 12
Ms. Harrison
Period 4

I have been to England before, and I have zero interest in going again with my school because I have no friends and spending a week away from home where no one but tour guides and teachers will talk to me (occasionally) is not my idea of fun. Even though I know my father will give me Xanax to deal with the twelve-hour flight, "better living through chemistry," he always jokes, there aren't enough of those pills to stop my mind from obsessively repeating magical chants, hoping I hit on just the right combination of words to render me totally invisible while Sara and Heather sit huddled in the back of the tour bus whispering about how glad they are that they don't have my fat ass and red hair. Yeah, well they should be glad. My body is Rubenesque while the current fashion is Toothpick-esque, and centuries of scientific research have met their match with my hair. The Hubble telescope floats around in space, but not one product on the market is able to straighten and/or soften my hair. Go flippin' figure.

I would love to see Stonehenge and Bath and Stratford-upon-Avon. Those are places where a love of literature is acceptable because so many great authors wrote there that you still feel all their words floating in the air. I've only been to one place in the United States where I could feel words in the air and that was Gettysburg, and the words I felt were heavier and pricklier than the ones blanketing Stratford-upon-Avon. So that's really why I would want to go back to England. Maybe the invisible language would be enough to make me forget the thirty people in my senior class who I would be traveling with.

But not enough to forget about Jacob. He would be there, of course. He and Keira would both be there. I wish he were mean or something. But he isn't. I love him. Writing those words makes me hot. Admitting it makes me hot, makes me hotter. Am boiling as I type. May spontaneously combust. And even though I somehow wrote those three sizzling words seemingly against my will, I would deny it even if I were being held in Guantanamo Bay and admitting my love for him were the only thing that would release me. I'd rather stay imprisoned than have anyone know how much I love Jacob. I am just not going on the school trip.

SECRET ME-MOIR ENTRY 10/8
Secret #2 (#1 is that I love Jacob Kingston)

Assignment given by me for my eyes only

I think about all the girls in my class and honestly, I'd love to have any one of them write my name down on that slip of paper. Even the really mean ones. I wish I could hate them and say I would never want to be seen with any of them or that I would never, not in a million years, ever want to share a room with them on the school trip. But it's not true. I'd love for just one of them (even the ice queen, Heather) to be willing to share a hotel room with me for just one week. But they don't. In a movie I would get to have psycho powers, and after they spilled a bucket of blood on me at the prom, I would have my revenge through Satan's hellish magic. But in real life I don't even hate them. I just hate me.

*CLASS ASSIGNMENT * 10/9
Essay #4: The Class Trip

(What I did turn in along with a note begging Ms. Harrison not to make me read it aloud. I got a C+. I still had to read it aloud because she thought other students might want to hear about my England experiences. She was wrong. They used the time to yawn, roll their eyes, and doodle. Jacob paid attention. When I read the part about the horrible weather, Heather blurted out that global warming wasn't real and if I had the courage, I would have laughed in her face.)

Danielle Levine

English 12

Ms. Harrison

Period 4

It is very exciting that the class trip is to England this year; although, we aren't going until the beginning of March so I'm not sure why we are discussing this right now. However, thank God we aren't going in November, the most wildly unpredictable weather month in England since the new millennium, probably due to global warming. March should be lovely.

London is a wonderful city with more history and rich *ambience* than the strip-malled, strip-clubbed, fenced in dog-parked, crisscrossing freewayed city of Los Angeles could ever hope for. I have been to England five times. My whole family goes when my father has to give lectures about new medical procedures. While my dad works, my mom and I go to museums (I love the Tate Modern), and we take the train out of the city and into Bath and Stratford-upon-Avon. In Bath, I always think about Jane Austen and how great a character Elizabeth Bennet is. I own a bonnet that my aunt bought me in a vintage shop in England that is exactly what I think Elizabeth would have worn at one of the parties where she found herself face-to-face with Mr. Darcy. You can tell she loves Mr. Darcy right away, but she is so independent and fiery that there is no way she is going to let him know. But unlike life, which is why it's great to read books, everything works out for the two of them in the end.

Before the trip, we find out what Shakespeare play is being performed in Stratford, and then my mom and I read it on the flight over. I never have any idea what Shakespeare is talking about at first. But, I read the passages slowly, multiple times, and break them down into small bits (a helpful strategy for managing many of life's hard tasks, btw) and then wait for the meaning to rise in me, kind of like a burp. That technique is worth a try for anyone interested in really getting all the cool stuff that Shakespeare has to say. Now I can finish any quote my mom tries to throw at me. I can do this with the Brontë sisters, too. I am sure this information is about as thrilling and cool as having a snow globe obsession.

We go shopping at Harrods, and my mom buys me new

shoes because London gets the newer styles before Los Angeles does. She buys stilettos because they are for people who have good legs. I don't get those. Chuck Taylors are much better for a person like me. I have a closet full, a pair for every occasion. London is a very beautiful city and our class is lucky that this is where we are going. I'm sure my parents will make me go on this trip.

Teacher comments: *How exciting you've been to England five times. Please avoid tangential comments. I'm glad you will go on the trip.*

✳CLASS ASSIGNMENT ✳ 11/2
Technically Essay #3 but turned in after #4
Free Write

(What I did finally turn in, but really late, though, because I forgot about it. I got a D. I would hardly call this assignment "free.")

Danielle Levine
English 12
Ms. Harrison
Period 4

On Halloween, while most of my classmates dressed as monsters, vampires, and ghouls (a bunch of bloody messes), I am sure you are the only person who got that I came as Elizabeth Barrett Browning. My hair falls naturally into tendrils, so that didn't require much effort, and my aunt designed the corseted dress I wore. She gave it kind of a modern flair by having the skirt lay flatter than the 1800s called for, but that was so I didn't look too freakish at school. (But why should I have cared? James just splashed himself with fake blood and called that a costume. So gross. I have no idea what he was going for.) Also, my father runs around our house forever saying to my mom and me, "How do I love thee? Let me count the ways." You see, my costume had layers of personal meaning. So, when James mauled me and said, "Whoa, that dress is incredible and so weird at the same time," he got fake blood all over my aunt's hard work. Also, after that, people thought I was the bride of Frankenstein. Not an image I want following me throughout the year. It was horrible. I'd like to end this essay with a plea. *PLEA-se*, let's not have any more dress-up days at school. Thank you.

Disappointing teacher comments: *This is not an academic essay. It is a rant.*

Essay #5: My Worst Day

(What I don't turn in, but what is, indeed my second worst day ever.)

Danielle Levine
English 12
Ms. Harrison
Period 4

First off, Ms. Harrison, I don't know how you came up with this essay topic, but I fear it is from the parent meeting you had on Friday that turned into the absolute worst day of my life. So maybe this essay title is a tribute to me and, in which case, you are a total bitch for using my pathetic life for your purposes so you don't have to think of a really good essay subject like "Your Ideal Lover" or "Your Life After Plastic Surgery" or something really juicy like that.

My nearly worst day ever, not to be repeated, was the family night at school where Ms. Harrison and the principal gave a talk about the school trip to London. Everyone was there. Everyone. Even Jacob Kingston and that is why this day was really, really nearly the worst day of my life. The meeting started off fine with Ms. Harrison talking about all the things we would be doing on the trip (Big Ben, the Tate Modern, Westminster Abbey, etc.). And then Heather Hane's mom, who is a hateful cow, asked Ms. Harrison how the roommates for London would be determined. (I roomed with Heather on last year's trip to Canada.) Ms. Harrison explained that process to Heather's mom about how the kids wrote down who they wanted to room with and she would take that under advisement, but then, ultimately, she would make the final decision about who would room with whom since she's been coordinating the junior and senior trips for years now. This conversation followed, which I have since *emblazoned* in my memory, but not in any glorious way as the definition implies.

> **Heather's mom:** Well, last year my daughter did not get to room with who she wanted to, and it was quite uncomfortable and really ruined the trip for her.
> **Ms. Harrison:** I'm sorry to hear that, but we don't spend that much time in the rooms, and I think everyone is capable of getting along with his or her roommates, whoever they will be, for one short week.
> **Heather's mom:** I'm just saying that last year, Heather was pulled aside and asked if she would room with someone who she really didn't want to room with and she did it, even though she didn't want to, because she is a good person, and I just think that she served her time, and this year she should be able to room with someone who she wants to room with.
> **Ms. Harrison:** You know, Mrs. Hane, I think we are

going to have to talk about this at a different time.

Heather's mom: We pay a lot of money for these trips, and I just don't want my daughter to be miserable again this year.

My dad: Well, Mrs. Hane, last year I think my family paid for your daughter to go on the trip because you claimed financial hardship! So . . .

Principal: Dr. Levine, I think that is uncalled for . . .

Yeah, the principal stepped in to yell at my dad, but didn't once step in to stop Mrs. Hane from ruining my life right then and there. I melted inside every time Mrs. Hane opened her mouth because the crowd was listening to her so intently. Even Sara, who had been crouched in the corner with a migraine, stood up to get every word of Ms. Hane's complaint. I felt sorry for Ms. Harrison because I knew she was just trying to do her best, but most of all I felt sorry for me because I just wanted to die.

I didn't know that Ms. Harrison had to beg Heather to room with me last year, and I didn't know I had ruined her trip. I brought books and stayed quiet on purpose and didn't talk to her unless she talked to me. I didn't undress in front of her, so she didn't see my fat, ugly body and get embarrassed. I did everything I could, but obviously, that didn't do anything. I sat in the auditorium and mustered all the strength I had not to cry. But it wasn't enough. When the meeting ended my father went to talk to Ms. Harrison, and I ran to the car and almost tripped right over Jacob who had to be able to see that I was crying. My furry black hat fell off my head, and I forced my dad to go back for it while I obsessively patted my head in the car because at that moment I just felt like my hat needed to be there, and I was freaking out. Jacob walked passed my car as I was smacking my head, and he looked at me like I was nutcase. Which, of course, is right on.

I am going to pretend like I hate Jacob Kingston instead of loving him (which will be a monumental task because he is built like the statue of *David*) so that every time I see him from now on I am not so humiliated. I wish he could melt and go away.

CLASS ASSIGNMENT 11/12
Essay #5: My Worst Day

(What I do hand in, and thank God Ms. Harrison does not make me read this aloud, but she does want me to meet with the school psychologist. C+)

Danielle Levine
English 12
Ms. Harrison
Period 4

My worst day was the day I was born. My parents are not what made it the worst day. My parents are wonderful. Anyway, as you know, I wasn't even born to my parents, which is really easy for anyone to see because I look nothing like them. My parents are very good looking. My parents adopted me from someone who I am sure looks just like me and was having a horrible life and just couldn't bear the thought of making it worse by having to raise a child while having a horrible life.

That day of my birth was my worst day because I was born on the wrong planet, in the wrong body, for no real good purpose that I can *ascertain*. (Thank you for teaching me that word. One thing I like about life on this planet is all the great words I get to learn in your class.) I'm sure on other planets life is not as ridiculous as it is here. In fact, I imagine that on other planets, people aren't actually in bodies so it saves a lot of hassles. That day I was born marked the stressful beginning of a very stressful life.

Teacher comments: *Sometimes we all wish we were never born; your whole life won't be like high school.*

Essay #6: Reflecting On My College Applications

(For this very honest assessment: C. What does this lady want from me?)

Danielle Levine
English 12
Ms. Harrison
Period 4

    Reflecting on the college application process is like trying to navigate your way through a hurricane. (I hope you like my simile.) I applied to three University of California schools and three state of California schools. I really only had to complete two applications online, one for the UCs and one for the states. This was not as simple as you might think.

    My mom sat with me as I did the applications because, like she said, it felt like you needed a master's degree in form-filling-out to do it. It was an OCD person's nightmare. I needed my mom because I kept checking every question and answer four times. If I didn't check each question four times and say the question and my answer out loud twice, then I couldn't move on. My mom yelled at me to stop doing that. I couldn't. Then, I repeatedly asked her how I was going to pack up all the things in my room and fit them in a dorm room. I told her I have to have my own room because I can't possibly share decorating space with someone. I started worrying that my postcards would get bent in the move. I also needed to know, right then, the exact dimensions of a dorm room, so I started measuring my furniture. She really lost it at that point.

I yelled at my mom for not hiring someone to do the applications for me like a lot of other kids in my class did. I put on my blue conductor hat and my black combat Chucks to gain some control.

My mom made me take a double dose of Adderall when all the yelling started, and I think that was a terrible thing for her to make me do. You shouldn't mess with your meds like that, and we didn't even check with my dad first before doing that because he was giving a lecture out of state, and I told my mom that she was giving me Munchausen syndrome by proxy because of these stupid applications. Then she told me I was being ridiculous because my Adderall dosage isn't that high, and she was trying to help me not hurt me. Then she got upset that my father tells me all about the weird conditions that people can get because I remember the things he says but apply the knowledge at the wrong time. I hope you are coming to understand what a pain this process was.

Because my mom will not listen to me complain about how lucky the other kids in my class are, I'm going to tell you. The kids who get college counselors to do their applications are soooooooo lucky. Sara is the luckiest because her mom and a counselor applied to all her schools, and she doesn't even know where she applied, and she said it's going to be like

Christmas for her when she finds out. I wish it were going to be like Christmas for me, too, but it won't be because I'm just so anxious about whether or not I even did the applications correctly that I don't care where I get accepted. Also, I'm taking the SATs again soon and the thought of that gives me hives. (Now I have ADD, OCD, Munchausen syndrome by proxy, and eventually, hives.)

I'm so worried that when I take the SATs again, I will do what I did on my Algebra II test last week. I saw question #1 and thought "What if I just stare at this page for the whole test?" "What if I just think about staring at this test the whole time while I'm staring at this test the whole time?" "What would happen if I stared at this test the whole time?" "How would someone intervene?" "Would they intervene?" "What will the score that I get on this test really mean?" "Why does this test matter when it just gets thrown away and turns into garbage?" "How come it means something now but doesn't have any meaning in a month after the grades are posted and it does become garbage?" "Why did we make up this system?" "Who did make up this system?" "Why can't I stop coming up with questions in my mind?" Anyway, you get the point.

Teacher comments: *Stay calm. If you are going to be up for the challenges that college present, you have to be up for the challenges that filling out the applications present. Avoiding those challenges is not a good idea.*

✳CLASS ASSIGNMENT ✳ 11/18
Essay #7: The Importance of Rules

(My least favorite essay topic to date. The whole class, all thirty of us, had to write this essay after a small group of people were late coming back to the bus after seeing an exhibit at the Santa Monica Pier. Heather, Sara, James, and John should have had to write this essay and the rest of us should have just made fun of them, but that didn't happen because they are popular and that's just one of the important rules of life: popular people have a get-out-of-jail-free card, which is literally true for O.J. Simpson, according to my father. Credit for completion on this one.)

Daniel Levine

English 12

Ms. Harrison

Period 4

   Rules are super important. Without rules, there would be chaos. Because some people at the History of Thanksgiving exhibit today didn't follow the rules, there was chaos. Heather, Sara, James, and John (two popular couples, as you know) spent way too much time fooling around on the pier and then *sauntered* back late to the bus carrying French fries. The rest of us had to wait on the bus, and Ms. Harrison (as you know) was really angry because first she couldn't find the missing kids because of all the tourists walking about and all the swooping seagulls, but also she was afraid we would hit rush-hour traffic and then not get back to school on time. Kids breaking rules was going to cause the teacher to break a rule, which I guess is that if you take kids on a field trip, you have to get them back to school before the bell rings.

As a woman of sorts myself, I am glad there are rules, honestly. Sometimes when I am really upset I want to do some truly socially unacceptable things that I would carry out if there weren't real life consequences for my urges. So rules are good to protect me from doing things that would harm others or me or just embarrass me. For instance, last month there were about two days that I just wanted to cry over everything.

I was shopping with my mom at the grocery store, and this model woman and her beautiful daughter came up to talk to my mom. I guess my mom sold them a house, and so they were very friendly. When my mom introduced me to them as her daughter, they both had this sort of shocked look on their faces like they couldn't believe I was Evelyn's daughter. I pulled my stretchy hat down over my eyes to try to avoid their gaze, but my mom gave me a nudge, which meant she wanted me to try to be social. I'm sure it is hard for my mom in situations like this. She didn't know when I was a tiny, cute baby that I would grow up to be an ugly teenager. Anyway, these chicks really were disgusted with me, and I just wanted to punch them in the face, and I think I might have if there weren't laws to prevent me. (Although, there should be laws preventing people from looking at you in a disgusted way just because you aren't pretty.)

I imagined myself grabbing a bunch of food from the frozen food aisle and whizzing it at their perfect little noses and breaking them. I wanted the girl to have to go to school with a big swollen nose and a big black eye. That really isn't a very nice thing for me to think. But thank goodness there are rules in this world and because of that I didn't mess up those women's faces.

Teacher comments: *Beauty is in the eye of the beholder, Danielle. You are too hard on yourself.*

SECRET ME-MOIR ENTRY 11/30
Secret #3: My F'd-Up Meeting with Marv

We had Thanksgiving break and I stuffed myself silly. It was awesome to see Aunt Joyce and spend the whole time watching Masterpiece Theater and old BBC videos, which inspired us to speak with British accents all weekend. I did not think that when I came back to school Ms. Harrison would remember that she wanted me to see Marv, the school psychologist. But apparently the woman has a memory like an elephant.

The day we got back to school, I had to wait outside Marv's office for everyone and their mother to see me. First, Sara walked by after being in the nurse's office, her second home, and as she limped by she piled all her brown hair on the top of her head as if its weight on her shoulders was simply too much to bear. She let out a sigh and gave me this obnoxious look of "just what are you doing here?" because, I swear, she has marked the counseling and nurse's offices as her private territory. So now I guess she thinks I'm trying to steal her medical staff. Hardly.

Jacob took some note to the front office and saw me sitting there wearing my gray fedora and he said, "nice hat," but what's terrible is that I was reading *Jane Eyre*, and Jacob is not stupid. I'm sure he found it laughable that someone like me would lose myself in such a novel. I will be no one's Jane Eyre. (Well, I might end up like the Jane Eyre of the first half of the novel, who works as a nanny and takes abuse from the dark and troubled hero. But I can't imagine that I'd ever reach her level of *redemption*.)

I finally got into Marv's cramped office and had to sit on the only chair available: a red one shaped liked a giant hand. So weird. The chair made me feel like a dwarf, but the small room made me feel like a giant. My equilibrium was way off. He sat behind his desk and didn't say anything forever. So awkward. I felt compelled to speak.

"So who is that hippie with the clown nose?" I asked about one of the framed posters on the wall.

"Oh, that's Wavy Gravy. You know him?" I shook my head. "He's an activist hero of mine. When I was a kid, this guy was fighting to make a better world. He got beat up by the authorities so often he decided to become a clown. What a genius reaction. Inspiring, right?"

I didn't understand but I said yes just so we could move on. I stared at my confused reflection in the giant peace-symbol mirror Marv had behind his desk and tried to change my expression to a look of intense interest. I picked up one of the pet rocks he had on his desk and nodded in approval. Who knows of what. I was improvising.

Marv finally said, "I know I'm not much of a hippie on the outside. Good haircut, collared shirts, and ties are the rules of the job, but inside, my heart is all Wavy Gravy."

"Mmm. Nice. I think I've had his ice cream."

From that strange moment, Marv commented on how *unique* it was that I italicize all the vocabulary words in my English essays. I let him think it was unique instead of telling him I have to or something bad might happen.

Then he saw my copy of *Jane Eyre* and complimented me on my high-brow literary tastes. He didn't know that when I read such stories, I lower the brow. I picture the heroine as a girl with rolls and rolls of fat on her stomach and cellulite on her thighs and the hero, Mr. Rochester in this case, likes her anyway. I know enough not to throw my crazy front and center like that on a first meeting. I actually said very little to Marv and thought I made a clean getaway, but when I got home, I found out he talked to Mom: I have to join a social skills class and start taking yoga. Damnit.

(Apparently, not my best effort. D)

Danielle Levine

English 12

Ms. Harrison

Period 4

This is a very broad topic, Ms. Harrison. I'm just saying. I've decided I'm going to tell you about something that happened to me recently with regard to movies. It stresses me out a little when I think about this incident, so I've put on my black combat Chucks while I write this essay because those give me a sense of control, albeit a false sense, I know.

I used to be allowed to order whatever films I wanted through my family's online subscription. I am not allowed to do that anymore. What happened is not even really my fault, but my parents don't see it that way.

I wanted to rent this Jake Gyllenhaal movie called *Brothers* after I heard Sara and Heather talking about how good it was. I had never heard of it, but the title made me think it was a nice family-type film. Also, I think Jake Gyllenhaal is super cute. He reminds me of a real life person, who, for reasons I can't explain here, will remain nameless.

So, I rent *Brothers*. Did you know that some American movies are remakes of movies made in other countries? I had no idea until this unfortunate incident. Oh, I better explain something else to you, too. I am not allowed to watch super-violent movies. My parents are against me doing that, and, quite frankly, I'm just not the kind of person who can handle seeing disturbing, violent images on film. That's a good FYI for you in case you were planning to show us any slasher films in class. LOL.

Brothers comes in the mail and I start watching it, and, to my shock, it's in Swedish or Danish or some interesting language like that. I'm thinking, whoa, Jake Gyllenhaal is way smarter than I thought. So, I'm watching this movie and Jake is nowhere to be found, but I assume he's coming up somewhere. But, some SUPER-upsetting moments happen while I'm waiting for his entrance. Just one example: one guy in the film is forced by a psychopath to kill his cellmate or else he will be killed himself. That is an impossible situation to be in and so horrific. I had a meltdown. I froze like a deer caught in headlights and then started breathing rapidly, and the movie kept playing and Jake never showed up, and I was watching the scenes while crying and stuff, but my eyes would not unglue from the screen no matter what. Eventually, I curled up in a fetal position. On top of that, I had left a baked potato in the oven and it was burning in there and I wasn't even aware of that because of the trauma of the film.

My dad came home from work and saw the smoke in the kitchen and what was happening to me, and he sent me to my room. He got emotional over all my emotions. Bye-bye ordering-my-own-movies privileges.

Jake Gyllenhaal is in the American version of that movie, but I am not allowed to see it. My father had a long talk with me about reading the descriptions of the movies *before* they are ordered. That's what responsible adults do. My father is very in to me behaving "like a responsible adult" and learning to understand myself better and knowing what I can tolerate. Believe me, I'm grateful that he is always trying to help me in this way, but it is stressful because, obviously, I don't always live up to expectations.

So, then, I went through my parents' movie collection and found *Brokeback Mountain* and watched that because I was in a Jake Gyllenhaal mood. If you haven't seen that movie, OMG, it's depressing. I cried during that one, too, but I did it quietly and watched it on my computer in my room surrounded by my hats, my snow globes, and all the postcards on my headboard. After the movie it took me days to hang my hats back on my wall in the right order and to categorize the snow globes as I wanted them. But, the effort was time well spent.

Mainly, that movie made me think about an article I read in an entertainment magazine. While his male costar was getting to fall in love and have a baby during the filming of that movie, Jake was breaking up with his girlfriend. That had to be really hard to handle in the moment, watching someone else be happy all the time. Jake couldn't have known then that his costar was destined for such an early and tragic death. He couldn't have conceived that life would do that to him. No one imagines such a thing. I am sure Jake is now walking around this planet ruined, and I ache for him. The wheel of fortune is *unfathomable*.

So, there's movie magic for you. These particular movie experiences sent me for a whirl, for sure.

Teacher comments: *Not the tone I was looking for. Please pay attention in class when I give the guidelines for the assignment or check them online before proceeding.*

SECRET ME-MOIR ENTRY 12/6
Secret #4: Too Secret to Title

(So secret that I am hot while writing it, will die if ever read by another soul.)

I have no right to love Jacob Kingston, and the only thing that makes it acceptable in my own mind that I have these feelings is that they physically hurt. I think about him and my chest tightens, I can't breathe, and I feel like I've been punched in the stomach.

Last year in U.S. history, our teacher assigned us partners to work with on a research project. Mr. Resurrection (that's really his name) paired me with Jacob. I didn't love Jacob then. I didn't love anyone.

On the first day of the project, while we were poring over the handouts, Jacob looked up from his stack and said, "You have really cool green eyes." That one sentence started all this pain.

Jacob is the most popular, good-looking guy in the class. He is dating the most *gregarious*, generous girl in the class, but she is not the most beautiful—that's Heather, the blond bombshell, who has told us a million times about how she's been photographed for magazines. Jacob's girlfriend, Keira, is tiny but athletic, and her short, thick black hair is a lovely contrast to her porcelain skin. Her cheeks and lips are naturally rosy, so she never needs makeup. Somehow, I love Jacob more because he loves Keira. I'm sure he loves how she laughs well and at all the right times, how her short hair can be styled in a million fun ways, and how she fits in everywhere. Keira includes people.

Last summer, I actually went to a pool party because a parent invited the entire class, and my parents forced me to go. I sat in a chair under a tree with my giant yellow sun hat tilted over my face for most of the day. When I was brave enough to look out from underneath its rim, I watched Jacob hold Keira on his shoulders in the pool while she shot everyone with a water gun. He was so careful with her, not wanting her to fall off or be uncomfortable. He held on to her so tightly. In that pool and all over campus, they appear to be one living being, the way couples are supposed to be.

Jacob is the quarterback of our football team, and God, that makes him even hotter. It's so embarrassing to admit this but I bought a San Francisco 49ers' snow globe because that is Jacob's favorite team. I kinda hide that one behind the other twenty-seven in my room because it doesn't fit in, and I don't want anyone to ask me why I have a football team snow globe. Although, I could always tell people that several members of

The Romantic Era were football players—it's true—and that's why I have that snow globe. That's good thinking.

Jacob has beautiful wavy brown hair that I stare at in every class because how can I possibly avoid looking at him when there are only a dozen kids in each class and Cruel Fate scheduled me in every one of Jacob's this year? Sigh. I would love to move my fingers through his hair; I picture doing that sometimes. His brown eyes are so big and kind and appear hungry for all there is to see. Someday, maybe my eyes will find a way to want to see all there is to see, too.

There are some days that I remember what Jacob said to me about my eyes, and I try to remember that for as long as I can instead of thinking about the thing I can't ever forget. Some feelings are so big they will swallow you whole. You have to do something to protect yourself from the swallowing.

The knot in my stomach is bigger than ever.

✻MENTAL HEALTH MISSIVE✻ 12/8

Letter #1 for the Commitment Hearing Committee (so they know what was the beginning of the end of any piece of sanity I had left in high school).

Dear Commitment Hearing Committee that is not currently real but could materialize should things get worse from here due to my social skills class.

A social skills class can really be of no benefit if everyone in the class has no _viable_ social skills. Hasn't some expert thought this through a little more fully? None of us is going to evolve into anything beyond our misfit selves if we have no one to _emulate_. I fear we will stay stuck as a sour group of potential.

I swallowed the lump in my throat for the entire two hours, and picked obsessively at loose threads on my red Chucks and my blue conductor hat, thinking just how far off course my life has gone that I've ended up here with these people in the basement of a dilapidated Presbyterian church whose membership is obviously dwindling. The fluorescent lighting made me feel like a criminal under interrogation.

I'll just list the stats as they exist at this point:

Charles—stiff as a board, bug-eyed, monosyllabic, possible hermaphrodite, grunge-band-group wannabe.

Megan—very pretty but seems to have no idea about that, stares at floor or inside her sweater at all times, picks her fingernails or unravels sweater, speaks so quietly I can never hear her.

Andy—smells awful, really awful, makes me want to gag, probably just needs to be told to shower regularly, get a hair cut, and wear something other than all black and he may be functional out in the world.

Iggie—makes things out of paper the entire time.

Daniel—most normal member of group. He has awesome black hair that is just a little too long. I think he keeps it that way on purpose because when he gets all passionate about what he is saying he jerks his head dramatically and flips his bangs out of his face. He wore a flannel shirt over a Che Guevera print tee, black Chucks, and was obviously pissed about being in this class: I like him for all those things. I kept staring at him. I'm sure he thinks I'm a freak.

At one point he said, "Look, life is what you make it and I feel the monastery offers an elevated existence that is actually more real than the synthetic bullshit Walmart-ized vibe of the twenty-first century . . . " Our group leader, Lisa, is constantly trying to get him to talk in the present about the details of his life, but he just won't. He's completely <u>obstinate</u>. Daniel is not a physically big guy. When we both stood up to stretch at the break, I noticed he was just an inch or two taller than me, like five nine or so, but his personality was well over six feet. I'm sure this class will do nothing for him, but he's at least entertaining.

It is clear to me that Lisa is in way over her head. She smiles constantly at all our <u>wan</u> faces while speaking from note cards about how we are going to work on "connecting with people" and "feeling comfortable with ourselves" while we learn to "embrace ourselves as social beings." Read the crowd, lady.

We sit in a circle in these lame white folding chairs. Against the wall there is a dusty table that has flyers about "surrendering to a higher power" and a plate of cookies, but I can't eat them because the entire room smells musty. Not appetizing. I start counting the yellowed, dirty tiles on the floor and become <u>acutely</u> aware that this room is used for an AA meeting after we are through, as if our future selves will be visiting to show us a vision of what is to come for all of us.

Suddenly, I just start thinking about how I'm at least twenty pounds overweight, how every bag of potato chips is a single serving bag to me, and how sitting on my ass for hours at a time is an Olympic sporting event in my world; I start obsessing on all the different flavors of potato chips I like, especially barbecue, and then I start thinking about all the brands of barbecue potato chips I like and how I don't like Pringles; how sometimes I see how small a bite I can take or how long I can keep one chip in my mouth before it dissolves, I actually time it; how I look for all the same size chips and keep them in groups according to size and amount of BBQ flavoring, and I realize I am having an OCD anxiety attack but cannot do anything to stop it and that's when I think that probably someday I will have to be committed to a mental facility of some sort and of how I will have to go home and write this letter to the committee so they will know I am at least <u>cognizant</u> enough to know I should be sent somewhere.

In the future, if someone looks into what might have caused my demise, these letters will be proof that this class was part of my fall into psychosis. That I was <u>prescient</u> about where I was going.

Lisa: Danielle, why don't you turn to Iggie and tell him something about what you would like to do in your spare time?

Me:

Lisa: Danielle, remember, there are no wrong answers to be given here. And be sure to look at Iggie and use his name when you address him because that is gracious and a sign that you are open to connecting with someone for conversation.

Me: Iggie, I think it would be cool if I had some really good ideas about what to do in my spare time so I didn't have to be here on a Tuesday night.

Daniel laughs.

What I'd like, actually, is a gigantic magical eraser that I could rub over everyone in the room and watch as their faces and bodies slowly turn into rubbery fragments that fall to the floor. Then I'd get a broom and sweep up their powdery remains and dump them into the ashtray cans that are everywhere in this church basement. Then for fun, I'd like to run out the door and keep running until my face is chapped by the wind. Maybe I would cry for a very long time because I just erased all the people who are most likely my kindred spirits, and I can only feel <u>disdain</u> for them.

CLASS ASSIGNMENT 12/12
Essay #9: Things I've Seen.

(Ms. Harrison wanted us to give a "rich and detailed account" of something "significant" we have seen. I pick a bad topic. D+)

Danielle Levine
English 12
Ms. Harrison
Period 4

I have seen things that will not be discussed here, and I have seen things that will be discussed here but probably shouldn't be, but you assigned the essay and so I'll leave your reaction up to you and call it your business. You should be aware that when you assign an essay topic like this to teenagers of the twenty-first century, you are going to get some interesting responses that go beyond descriptions of the lame holiday decorations at the mall or whatever. The world is not like it was when you were young. (Not saying that you are old, just saying the world is different, that's all.)

From across the street, I've seen my neighbor, a forty-year-old corporate executive, buy pot from this kid who drives a Hummer, which is an abomination to the planet, according to my father. My parents don't like our neighbor at all, but it's not because he buys weed from the Hummer-driving kid. They don't like him because he's living with a woman who is only twenty-two. Although my parents are very judge-not-lest-ye-be-judged kind of people, on this issue, they judge.

When I'm walking the dogs, I've seen this dealer sing songs from his car to alert Ken, the corporate executive neighbor guy, that his delivery has arrived. All the dogs bark when this is going down because they have instincts. Sometimes, the dealer gets out of his car and pees (I don't know if I can say that in this essay, but I did see that) on the lawn. The dogs all want to pee then, too, which can get kind of messy.

I've also seen my father walk across the street and speak to our neighbor. I'm only speculating here, but I'm pretty sure that my dad was talking to our neighbor about the inappropriate nature of his drug dealings when there is a teenager living across the street. It would be a lot funnier if what I had seen was my father buying weed off him. (JK)

Teacher comments: *Do not write about contraband. You are capable of description beyond what you demonstrated here; such a topic is beneath your intellect.*

✶MARV MISSIVE✶
Letter #1 from Marv

(I give him a B, mainly for effort.)

Danielle,
   Your teacher, Ms. Harrison, tells me that you are
a very good writer. She suggests that we may make
more progress together if we put our ideas into writing rather than talking. I thought it was an intriguing
idea since you seem hesitant about expressing yourself
in conversation when we are together. This is very
unorthodox, but I spoke with your mother, and she felt
it might be a good idea. She, too, lauded your writing
ability, and hey, you never know, our communications
back and forth may support the budding author within
you. What do you say?
   Marv

Letter #1 from me to Marv

(My attempt to humor him and validate the cashing
of his paycheck. I slide it under his office door.)

Marv,
   I do like to write. However, I have no idea what I
would write to you.
   Danielle

SECRET ME-MOIR ENTRY 12/14
Secret #5: The Pied Piper

Today I watched Jacob lead a pep rally with the whole school—
elementary, middle, and high school. It was chilly outside and I sat
shivering in a back row bleacher. The crisp air may have been one
reason I was shaking, but I think there were feelings I'm not sure
how to describe bubbling up from inside and shaking all my parts.

The rally was outside on the football field, and the student
council and the athletes went nuts with it. They got all the
people who live in the houses surrounding the school to sign
permission slips about noise so music could be pumped out of
huge speakers. A local radio station sponsored the event and a
DJ came. Keira wore the panther mascot suit, and even though
I didn't want to have this thought, she reminded me so much of

a friend I used to have. It was the way she was dancing around the crowd, her musicality, I guess I'd call it. When she swayed to the beat, her body looked like a letter *S*, my favorite letter. *S* is sophisticated, sexy, sultry—a seductress letter. When I dance, I am just a bouncing *O*. An *O* is an outcast letter. Anyway, she was popping in and out of the crowd and letting some of the young kids jump on her back. Watching her was what Ms. Harrison would call *sublime* because her grace was both beautiful and painful to experience. I teared up watching her.

Jacob was on the microphone the whole time, introducing the football players and leading cheers and the games. Whenever he asked for volunteers, like for the balloon toss or the pie-eating contest, practically the entire student body, three hundred people, raised their hands—everyone just desperate to get up and be near him.

After all the games, he let a bunch of fifth graders smash the remains of the whipped cream pies all over him, and he just laughed and embraced all the little guys who were eager to hug him. Everyone was cheering and laughing and throwing confetti and blowing noisemakers, and I sat quietly in a back bleacher being totally enamored of Jacob's charisma. That's the thing about him I can't escape. I, like everyone else, am pulled in by his charisma.

When the bell rang to signal the end of the rally, he couldn't shake the line of kids running behind him. And even though I physically veered away from his *devotees* on my way back to class, every other part of me was following his trail.

MARV MISSIVE 12/16
Letter #2 from me to Marv after I see him at the nutrition break and he asks again if I would consider simply writing down some things I think about.

(Marv, that's really vague. But I do it, and this is what he gets.)

Marv,

Recently I have thought about how difficult it is to go through life fat. My thoughts may be because the holidays are coming and my mom bakes like a fiend this time of year, and I have no willpower to resist her treats. Being fat is far more difficult than being a woman, or a member of an ethnic underclass, or a paraplegic, or a midget. I say this, not to diminish the difficulty of those minority groups, but to highlight the fact that those poor people can't help their positions, and so people cut them some slack.

When you are fat, people assume it is your fault. And even if it is, why does it have to matter so much? Ancient Samoans had it the best because the bigger the woman, the hotter she was. Los Angeles is no ancient Samoa, let me tell you. In this city, I'm a painful reminder of what the <u>svelte</u> could become should they neglect their pilates classes and regular plastic surgery appointments. On this campus that is so lovely, (seven perfectly painted Spanish-style stucco buildings, fifteen large transplanted trees, forty-five shrubs, eighty-four rosebushes—that's right, I counted—one guy constantly leaf blowing the place) I'm a real eyesore.

Lately, I've just been thinking about how much it sucks to be fat. Thank God it's winter and I can hide under some layers.

Danielle

AUNT JOYCE E-MAIL 12/16
E-mail #1 to Aunt Joyce, who I just desperately need to help me

Dear Aunt Joyce,

I know you are in New York on business and I know you are really busy, but I really need to talk to you about something, and I'm hoping you can just find time to read this and then give me advice that rescues me like you have always done.

I am hopelessly in love with someone I will never have. Don't even think about writing back with a phrase that starts "Oh, Danielle, you don't know that you'll never have him." Trust me, and just regard my awareness enough to know that he will never love me. And, by the way, he has a girlfriend, and the point isn't that he won't love me, the point is that I love him, and I wish I didn't and I don't know why life gives you these feelings that can't be reciprocated or acted upon. What the hell?

I don't want to talk to Mom about this because I can tell when she looks at me she still sees me like I'm eight, and I just don't want advice designed for an eight-year-old. Also, I'm just not sure Mom understands pain, and, don't take this wrong, but somehow I think you do.

Please just take these feelings I have, work some magic with them, and give them back to me in a way that is more manageable.

Your dorky niece, Danielle

AUNT JOYCE E-MAIL 12/16
E-mail #1 from Aunt Joyce, who always responds when I need her to

Ah, Sweet, Sweet Danielle,

How blessed you are to know love in this way, and you just so happen to be revealing it to me near the holiday that symbolizes miraculous birth. Your literary mind surely sees the significance. This is the emergence of great hope.

You feel love! That's terrific. Come on, girl. Look back a few years. Did you think you would thaw enough to let feelings of this sort foment? This is the magic of love. I know you wonder how I can speak with such authority while I remain single and childless, but those facts are not reflective of the true experience of love. Marriage and children do not always follow love. The feeling is the gift itself, so think about that. Look at how something so invisible can have such powerful effects. Doesn't that say something to you about the nature of reality? Perhaps all is not as you see it in your world. I'd bet my life it is not.

I love you, kid.
Your Forever Aunt Joyce

P.S. Listen to me when I tell you, your mother understands pain.

MARV MISSIVE
Letter #2 from Marv to me

Danielle,

I thank you for your candor. It is not easy to write
down the thoughts that fill the mind. I know that you
and your mother are taking a yoga class together, and I
think this is a wonderful thing. Being active can be just
the medicine you need. I can write about how I do not
see you as you see yourself, but that would not address
any of your feelings. Your feelings are valid to you right
now. I hope I can help you shift your perspective.
   Sincerely,
   Marv

*DANIEL E-MAIL ... very interesting new
heading* 12/19 E-mail #1 from Daniel, the
guy in social skills class

Hi, Danielle,

It's Daniel from that class. Obviously I got your e-mail
from the completely intrusive one that Lisa sent us all,
encouraging us to connect with each other outside of class.
I didn't know how she got our e-mail and I told my parents
I thought she was breaking the law by stealing my e-mail

address. My parents said they gave her my e-mail when they signed me up for the class. That is so like them. I'm contacting everyone because I think we should ambush Lisa in the next meeting about the way she runs these classes. What do you think?

✳ CLASS ASSIGNMENT ✳ 12/19
Essay #10: Things I've Felt

(Ms. Harrison seems to want to know everyone personally. How noble. B–.)

Danielle Levine
English 12
Ms. Harrison
Period 4

Ms. Harrison, for the last few days, I've "felt" this essay topic is somewhat intrusive. Feelings are private things. Also, the holidays can be hard for people, so to ask about feelings at this time of year may be considered insensitive by some. However, ultimately, I've decided to *defer* to your authority.

I have felt things in my life that are now contained and controlled by what I can only describe as spigots. I try to keep the spigots tightly shut most of the time in order to prevent a flood of emotion on my insides and to manage my day as sanely as possible. However, recently, one of my feeling spigots has loosened. It seems as if this particular feeling has activated a spigot, which is now turned to a permanently stuck position of full-throttle flow. This feeling just keeps flowing over every other feeling whose spigots are either much smaller or very tightly locked. While this spigot thing is really annoying in a lot of ways, it is *intriguing* in others.

For a long time all my spigots seemed to be turned off. They were apparently rusted shut. Feelings had nowhere to move about or spread out, so they just dried up, I guess. I couldn't even muster a trickle. I was blocked up and feelingless for a while. But now that I have this flooding gush of feeling about this thing I can't really expand upon here other than to say it involves an issue of the heart, I recognize there is just no stopping a feeling once the spigots start to turn. What I'm trying to say is that feelings are very powerful forces. They are spigot turners.

I'm wondering what effect this one loose spigot is going to have on the other spigots. I can only hope and pray that any other loose spigots will release positive feelings, things that might help me become a more interesting person. Although, I think by some accounts I may already be interesting but in a bubonic plague kind of way. The bubonic plague is very interesting.

Oh, also, I wanted to tell you that the other day when Heather commented in class "that which doesn't kill us makes us stronger" . . . as if she would know or have any idea about

Nietzsche . . . I wanted to tell her "That is total bulls**t. That which doesn't kill us just almost kills us." That's how I feel about that. Heather always gives me an ax to grind.

I'm sure now you are going to suggest that I see Marv because of this whole spigot thing and my animosity toward Heather, but I'll tell you upfront that I am seeing him already so you can save your time on that.

Teacher comments: *Very provocative, but don't write judgmental comments about your classmates. Using asterisks does not mean you are not using profanity!*

DANIEL E-MAIL 12/20
E-mail #1: I write back to Daniel

Daniel,

I saw that Lisa sent an e-mail, but I deleted it before I opened it. I don't think she'll listen to us. She's a woman on a kamikaze mission.

Danielle

E-mail #2: Daniel writes back to me

Thanks for writing me back. You were the only one who did. I like your idea of deleting all her e-mails rather than my tactic of reacting to them. I'll have to get revenge some other way. Hey, have a good holiday.

CLASS ASSIGNMENT 1/9
Essay #11: A Picture Is Worth a 1000 Words

(I did not enjoy this essay topic, and yet, B+.)

Danielle Levine
English 12
Ms. Harrison
Period 4

Welcome back from the winter holiday, Ms.Harrison. I hope it was nice for you. I enjoyed hibernating during this break, lots of sleeping and reading.

Yes, a picture is worth a thousand words, I guess. There are a few that come to my mind and when I see them, epic stories are evident in an instant. Sometimes pictures even evoke sounds like a haunting oboe or something.

I like words more than pictures.

I don't have a camera. My parents bought me one for my birthday, but when I took pictures and thought about looking at them, I instead tossed the camera in the L.A. river. Then I had to work to pay my parents back for the money I wasted. It was a whole big thing. But if I want to look at some kind of captured image, I have snow globes for that.

I don't care if pictures are worth a million metaphorical words. I like real words. I should have been born in another era where people wrote letters and socialized over lemonade and a game of cards or a few cigars and talked about life's pertinent experiences while being shrouded in mystery under elaborate hats and layers of clothing. All their talk floats away along the path of smoke. Maybe remembered but really gone. Each person can keep what they want.

I see most photographs today and all I can think about is newspaper articles, grieving, and a frozen moment in time. Photographs are cruel that way. A photograph captures a moment of truth that can't be undone and makes it live on and on and on and on. They are reprinted, reloaded, posted, downloaded over and over and over again. They resurface and wound.

Teacher comments: *Some beautiful ideas here. I really think Marv is helping you.*

MARV MISSIVE
Letter #3 from Marv to me

<u>Probing</u> too deeply for my taste

Danielle,
    I read your essay about photographs. It was interesting.
Do you want to write more about that?
    Just wondering,
    Marv

MARV MISSIVE
Letter #3 from me to Marv

What he deserved in return

Dear Marv,
    NO.
    Danielle

MARV MISSIVE
Pathetic letter #4 from me to Marv

What I felt forced to write to Marv because Stella is
a crazy therapist.

Dear Marv,
   Well, sorry about the <u>curt</u> previous letter. Apparently you called my mom because she just called me
and said I have to go back to my crazy ex-therapist
Stella if I don't "open up" to you. So annoying. Look,
I really don't want to write about stuff that you
already know about from my file. I feel like your
asking me is just some kind of game to get into my
head, which is my business. Things are neatly organized in there. If I write to you about these things, it
may disorganize my filing system.
   Danielle

MARV MISSIVE
Letter #4 from Marv to me

Marv is smarter than I thought.

Danielle,
   I can understand that you've compartmentalized things

61

in order to cope. However, I would ask you to really think about how that is working for you. Is it working for you? Do you feel content?

　　With understanding,

　　Marv

MARV MISSIVE
Letter #5 from me to Marv

After a few days of thought and knowing I don't want to go back to Stella

Marv,

　　I would not say the "method to my madness" is a complete success. However, I cannot undo it at this time. I keep things stored away that must be stored away. When I write about them it loosens the spigots that have kept a hold on them. Please respect this. Turning a knob to full-throttle "<u>on</u>" could mean I can't get out of bed. How would that work for you?

　　Danielle

MARV MISSIVE
Letter #5 from Marv to me

Marv finally gets it.

Danielle,
   Understood. I have a feeling those spigots will loosen over time when you are ready for them to.
   Marv

AUNT JOYCE E-MAIL 1/13
E-mail #2 to Aunt Joyce, who can manage this <u>excavating</u> of my brain better than anyone

Dear Aunt Joyce,

I hope that the fashion show in New York was a smashing success and that you also had some time to visit some vintage shops for us. Things are a little *unwieldy* here. My mom is insisting I "see" this therapist at school; although, I don't have to actually see him. I just have to write back and forth to him. But I know what he wants. He wants what I've tied up and left neatly in the back of my brain. This e-mail is not for you to psychoanalyze me. Ms. Harrison, my parents, and Marv are doing that. I just want you to tell me if you have anything in the back of your brain that you've tied neatly in a bow and would like to leave there. Just tell me you have something like that.

P.S. Remember, anything you find for me clothing-wise needs to fit my enormous size 12 body.

AUNT JOYCE E-MAIL 1/15
E-Mail #2 from Aunt Joyce. She hides
something in her mind, too.

Danielle,

I will share something with you, and then after you are done reading it, I will ask that you delete it, so it can go back to living "tied neatly in a bow," as you describe it, in the back of my mind. I'm not sure how your parents will feel about me sharing this information with you, but I want you to have it, and I want you to understand it.

Seventeen years ago, the year your parents adopted you, I had an abortion. Now, have whatever reaction you choose to that. You won't be thinking anything I haven't already thought about my choice or myself. It's not something you let go.

Your mother was very angry with me—she knew pain—

because she had been trying for so long to get pregnant with you, and when it happened for me under very complicated circumstances, she couldn't understand why and how I could end this life. I also believe she was very upset that life could work this way. And I understand her perspective. She wanted a child so badly. I didn't. What sick forces were at work here, she must have thought.

During an especially virulent fight that I had with your mom, she begged me to have the baby so she could adopt it. It seemed like such a simple solution to her and something that, in her mind, the universe had worked out. But, Danielle, very little in life ever works so simply. I had gotten pregnant from a man whom I deeply loved but who was married. (Again, have whatever reaction you choose to that. Ditto, the above sentiments. You won't be thinking anything I haven't already vetted in therapy.) I was twenty-four years old, and child that I was, I loved this man the way I knew how to at the time. Danielle, you will love people in your life and the circumstances of that love will not fit into a neatly designed framework. You may not like it, but you will take it, or, at least, I hope you will. For all the pain, regret, and shame, I cannot change one moment of the affair or the decision I ultimately made.

It took years for your mom to forgive me. When you were gifted to them, I watched every minute of your coming-of-age thinking I could have had a son or daughter walking right alongside you. What might this child have offered you? But, had I had this child and allowed your parents to adopt him/her, then you wouldn't be with us at all. That is not an option any of us can accept. And so, it is you, your existence, your presence in my life that has helped to heal this situation for me. You mean so much to me, and now you know even more why. You are the child we are meant to have. Yours is the life that is meant to be here.

I hope this story is not more than you were bargaining for.

Your Forever Aunt Joyce

P.S. I have clothes for you, but in a size 8; you are a size 8, girl.

AUNT JOYCE E-MAIL 1/16
E-Mail #3 to Forever Aunt Joyce

Forever Aunt Joyce,

I am just so über-sad that you ever had to be so distraught. I can't imagine what all that was like, so I wouldn't even start to judge you. Boy, you really have had problems.

After I read your e-mail, I held the snow globe you bought

for me in Paris that time we went together, the one with the street scene by the Moulin Rouge. I shut my eyes, shook it, and held it close to my heart. Maybe you felt the love I sent you.

I deleted your e-mail, but I had to add it to my senior year me-moir binder first, but don't worry, no one will ever read it. You remember I keep all my life's important writings in individual sheet protectors in a locked binder wrapped in a pillowcase in a box under my bed. Your secret is very safe.

I'm just so selfish on some level because what stuck with me more than all the bad stuff you had to go through was the fact that I am really important to you. I'm so confused about what it is about me that is worth that kind of care. I just looked in the mirror for a bunch of minutes to see if I could see it, and I couldn't. I don't see the *me* that you see. I wish for just a little bit I could climb into you and then you could climb into me and then we could tell each other what we saw there. I really think that is the only thing that could help me feel better.

Also, I think it might be awful that a part of me is glad that you have something you keep hidden in the back of your mind tied up in a little bow. But, I have to tell you, there were a few times when I've looked into your eyes, and I saw that there was something messy about you. Don't be mad at me. It made me love you. (Also, your kind of messy does not make you ugly in any way.)

XOXOXO.
Danielle

✳CLASS ASSIGNMENT✳ 1/23
Essay Assignment #12: Something Beautiful

(Ms. Harrison is unable to see the real beauty I put forth here. And I even included parenthetical documentation, like we were working on in class! Poor Ms. Harrison! B-.)

Danielle Levine
English 12
Ms. Harrison
Period 4

Ms. Harrison, I really feel like I have to explain myself first before I get into the meat of this essay. I am going to write about something that at first is not going to seem beautiful at all, and I don't want you to think I'm crazy and don't know the difference between beautiful and ugly because believe me I do. But I have a father who told me that sometimes things we think are beautiful end up hideous and other things that we think are "lackluster," as he says, end up really shining. (I feel like one of those "lackluster" things sometimes. I hope someday I end up shining.) Anyway, I don't think I personally know about this shining business yet, but my dad is smart and I trust I will someday really get what he means. (There are a lot of things that people I respect say or write that I sort of get but not fully. Frustrating.)

My father told me about this news story that happened a while ago to the Amish people. He is very in to sharing *poignant* information with me. He said that a deranged man wandered into a schoolhouse in the Amish community and killed all these young girls. (This is NOT the beautiful part.)

My father told me that in a follow-up story in the news, we all got to learn how this community publicly forgave the man who did this to all those girls, who took all those girls from their families, who cut their lives so short. At first, I was mad at my dad for telling me this story even though he told me that "knowledge is power," and we must be open to hearing about difficult topics so we can grow. However, my point was: How could those people forgive that man? How could they forget about those girls' lives like that? My father said forgiveness does not entail forgetting about the people who are lost, but at the moment I was in no condition to process his point. I don't want to get into all the details of how this conversation went down at my house because I actually got super upset. Even my housekeeper, Martha, ended up in tears, and she is usually very *stoic*; I have the hardest time figuring out what makes her tick because she usually never shows any emotion about anything. (Figuring out what to get her for Christmas is impossible; I think we just give her cash.)

Anyway, the point is, eventually, I opened my mind just a little bit about what a miracle forgiveness can be if you can actually do it. I'm not really there yet, but I am at the point where I can be completely amazed at someone's ability to do it and recognize it as something beautiful. It is beautiful, I've come to realize (with help from my father) because it "is a sane choice under insane circumstances." (Doug Levine)

Forgiveness instantly stops the crazy energy that keeps people violent, that keeps stuff ugly, that makes pain grow. (Ibid) Forgiveness helps people who grieve. "The quality of mercy is not strained. It droppeth as the gentle rain from heaven upon the place beneath. It is twice-blessed: it blesses him that gives and him that takes." (Shakespeare) My father reminded me of that quote from *The Merchant of Venice*, which I saw one year in Stratford. It's not one of my favorite plays, but, still, when I realized how Shakespeare factored into this whole forgiveness thing, I saw how beautiful this Amish act of forgiveness really was. They really had an enormous thing to forgive and they did. I really need to learn from them.

So, I think they are beautiful and their forgiveness is beautiful even though I still realize I am nowhere near that beautiful or capable of forgiveness yet. I still let things bother me a lot.

Teacher comments: *The topic of this essay is wonderful, but*

*you are all over the place with it. You needed a printed news
story to reference, not your father's summary of it.*

DANIEL E-MAIL 2/14
E-Mail #3 from Daniel

Hey, I love your hair. I was thinking of putting some deep red
streaks in my hair, like your color. I don't know if it will show
up because my hair is so dark but would you mind telling
me what hair color you use? I'd prefer if you e-mail me back
about this because it's a weird thing to talk about in front of
other people. I'm just looking to do something that will shock
my parents. Happy Valentine's Day.

DANIEL E-MAIL 2/14
E-Mail #2 from me to Daniel

Daniel,

I don't dye my hair. I'm just naturally stuck with this color all
over my head.

Danielle

Wow, you're lucky. I think I'll just get a piercing instead of dyeing my hair.

SECRET ME-MOIR ENTRY 2/25
Secret #6 WTF

During the nutrition break today, I was sitting outside at the blue table by the library, the one where I like to chip off all the paint. It gives me something to do besides just reading, and it passes the time. On days when I think I'll have time to sit there, I wear my blue Chucks. They match the paint perfectly. I've been chipping this one spot pretty consistently all year trying to make it look like the skyline of New York City. My artwork had to stop when Keira plopped herself down next to me.

"I'm totally unprepared for the Algebra II test. Did you study for it?" she asked.

"I did, but, for that class, I generally resort to prayer. My brain is like a sieve when it comes to math."

"Prayer. Good idea. I need all the help I can get. I have to keep at least a B in this class or who knows what I'll do for college."

"You'll get in to college. You're what the admissions people see as a 'full package.'"

"Aw, you're nice." Keira started nervously flipping through her math notes when . . .

Enter disaster in female form.

"Hey, Heather. Did you study for Algebra II?" Keira asked her.

And then Heather launched into this über-irritating tirade that I couldn't possibly have memorized, but it went something like this: "Are you kidding? No. I'm too upset to study for that. James is all obsessed with learning this new soccer play, and he said I'm annoying him and all over the place with my needs or whatever, and he yelled at me to chill and I'm, like, chill? I'm always super chill, but he said 'uh-wrong' and I thought, well, maybe I'm not, so what. And then I tried to talk to Sara about this, but she's lying down in the grass by the quad because her head is hurting, and she told me to go away. I guess I'm a bug to everyone today or something. So I thought I'd buzzzzz over here, ha. Bzzzzzzz. Hey, Danielle, you're on Adderall, aren't you?" she asked as she lifted the straw fedora off my head like she owned it.

"Yeah." Shut up! What was I doing?

"Great. Can I have one?" Heather asked as if they were M&M's.

"Okay." I am possessed by a demon.

"Awesome."

But then I looked through my purse and realized I didn't have my medicine with me. I never do. I take it at home. So I had to tell her I didn't have it, and I looked like a scared freak and then she said, "Of course you don't have it. Shit. You always disappoint." And then she crushed my hat back down on my head as she walked away.

Keira said something about how now she could study without the chatterbox bugging her, and I picked at the paint on the table so hard that I made the skin under my fingernails bleed.

My own comment to myself: You're a moron.

AUNT JOYCE E-MAIL 2/28
E-mail #4 to Forever Aunt Joyce

Dear Aunt Joyce,

So we are getting ready to go to England with the class. The entire class, mind you. Mom took me shopping and bought me some clothes I don't want that look hideous on me. I don't want to travel around England with a bunch of kids who can't stand me, who talk to me only when they want something from me, who miss the bigger picture always, and who make me generally feel like a loser. Can you take me to the airport and pretend like you drop me off on Saturday but really you take me home with you and I just hide out in your condo? I won't leave the premises. My parents will never know. I swear. When we get to the airport, I will fake cancer or the stomach flu or hysteria so my teachers let me leave . . . I won't even have to fake the hysteria.

PLEASE!!!!!!!!!!

Desperate Danielle

AUNT JOYCE E-MAIL 2/28
E-Mail #3 from Aunt Joyce, who does not come through in a pinch

Danielle,

I will drive you to the airport. I was planning to go with you
and your parents anyway to take pictures of this big event.
No, you cannot hide out in my condo. You are hiding out
enough in your own life, and I want you to step forth. You
are living far too much in the realms of your head. That is
an ugly, mean, scary place to be. I am not just saying your
head is nasty, everyone's head is. You need to vacate that
premise immediately and start living in your heart. Your heart
is a much nicer social venue. Our mind is a crazy nightclub
of cacophonous sound filled with strange images and one-
night stands: our mind tells us lonely, loveless tales that leave
us frightened but really have no lasting power, like Mark that
graphic designer I met at a rave who told me that he once
woke up in a crack den in New York wielding an ax. I should
have known then, but, alas, you know the rest. . . . Anyway,
the heart is the symphony that supplants this noise. It knows.

It knows truths beyond this realm, but we can only find those things if we listen, if we step into its melody. You, girl, by no real fault of your own, are shutting out the music of the heart.

And, you know how I know all this? Because you are right, I have lived through mess and it has made me wise.

Did you ever consider trying to connect with some of these people that you view as cretins? If not, perhaps this trip will force that to happen. Sometimes our best decisions are made for us. Get packing! I bought you a pair of Chuck Taylors that have a Union Jack design. I'll bring them to the airport.

Love you,
Your Forever Aunt Joyce

AUNT JOYCE E-MAIL 2/28
E-Mail #4 to Annoying Aunt Joyce

Joyce,

I am beyond pissed at you. I am being therapist-ized by too many people. You are the place I turn to for acceptance and agreement. WTF?? You don't go to school with these people. You don't know. Also, life is just grand for you, and you can embrace the luxury of "living from your heart" because your delicate organ is cased perfectly in a size two body! My heart can barely be found beneath the rolls and rolls of fat that cover it the fuck up!! Also, in my heart is that horrifically painful love for that boy I told you about, and so why on God's scorched earth would I want to live there? It is a frickin' minefield of despair, to be perfectly honest. My head is at least logical. It knows how crazy I am, how crazy everyone else is, how insane it is to lust, that's right, lust after Jacob. I think my head is a dandy residence. There are locks on the door. Keep out!!!!

AUNT JOYCE E-MAIL 2/28
E-Mail #5 from an Apologetic Aunt Joyce

Sweet Danielle,

I am sorry if what I said was not what you wanted to hear. It's fine. Keep up residence in that head of yours. When you get tired of the property tax you will move into a more desirable location. Until then, I will love you as is. See you Saturday!

I just love you.
Your Adoring Aunt Joyce

AUNT JOYCE E-MAIL 2/28
E-mail #6 to Aunt Joyce

Joyce,

Good job extending a lame metaphor.

Danielle

AUNT JOYCE LETTER

Letter I give to Aunt Joyce at the airport just in
case I die in a plane crash. She takes a billion pictures
to go along with this letter. I feel like James and the
Giant Peach—me being the peach—dressed in the
orange sweater my mom made me wear on the plane.
The Union Jack Chucks don't match the sweater at
all, but I still wear them.

Dear Joyce,
   If I come home alive from this trip, then everything
I write in this letter is null and void and our rift will
continue. In the unlikely event of a water landing . . . I
want you to have these words.
   You have been the truest, lovingest (made-up
word, but works in this case), most important person

in my life. I am so grateful for you. I forgive you for not letting me stay at your condo even though because you wouldn't let me stay at your place I was killed in a terrible plane crash. I hope you don't spend too many years hating yourself for that decision. Fate is fate. Mainly, I just want you to know that you have helped me so much, and I will find every way possible to visit you from the afterlife. It is my hope that from that realm I will have a greater understanding of how to live from my heart and not my neurotic, OCD head.

I love you no matter what.
Danielle

JOURNAL FROM A PLANE 3/1
#1 Airborne journal . . . can't believe the drama going on around me . . . am writing at a feverish pace . . .

We've been in the air for over four hours. I am sitting right across the aisle from the bathroom. This is the worst possible seat for an twelve-hour plane ride because by hour nine the stench will be unbearable. I know this because I've been on a thirteen-hour flight to China and after people eat and drink for a few hours they let go of any and all *decorum*, especially the men. This one guy I saw puked all over the bathroom door while he was trying to hit on this totally uninterested and brain-dead woman in line behind him, who was like a size zero with really huge fake boobs. After he puked he just kept complimenting her on all her junk. It was beyond gross. Danielle, stop thinking about that and get back to the drama at hand.

Something terrible has happened, and it's psycho how great I think it is. Sara is super sick! First, she took a bunch of Advil because she has cramps. Keira was walking the aisles looking for more Advil for Sara because she was in so much pain. Keira is a good friend. (Probably another reason Jacob likes her. Shut up, Danielle.) Sara whined about the pain all through check-in and even her own boyfriend, John, was rolling his eyes at her. Jacob wheeled her giant suitcase through the long line because (I want to believe) Sara is just so annoying because of her low tolerance for everything, and Jacob wanted her to shut up about how much her cramps hurt and how hard it was to maneuver her oversized leopard-print suitcase through the line. (Jacob is a saint. Self, stop thinking about Jacob.)

After Sara took all that Advil, I guess she ate a bunch of stuff. I don't know what, but now she is "having some sort of reaction" according to one of the flight attendants who ran by.

I can see Sara up ahead of me just a few rows. She keeps falling out of her seat and tossing things from her lap onto passengers next to her while all these people are coming and going trying to figure out what's wrong with her.

A bunch of tampons just fell out of her purse and rolled

down the aisle. Some British flight attendant guy had to pick them up. He was not amused.

Oh my God, she's trying to stand up. She fell down! The woman next to her seems really frustrated even though that is not at all the PC way to react when someone is sick right by you, but I can't help it, I love the woman who is annoyed with Sara. Love her. Wait, whoa, it looks like Sara can't keep her eyes open. I think this might be serious.

Keira just appeared from around the corner of the flight attendant station. I think she's looking for Jacob. Now Ms. Harrison just walked past me and she looks really worried.

Now I'm starting to get worried.

OMG.

What if my mean thoughts about Sara had a force of their own? What if they were psychically projected as a biologically destructive black cloud? Just what if? What if all my ill will literally made her diseased. I'm panicking here. I have to go lock myself in the bathroom. Gotta get to a safe zone.

So I went to the bathroom in the back of the plane and stayed in there forever because I overheard this conversation outside the door while I was in there. (Now, I'm an eavesdropper on top of unleashing a biological black cloud of destruction.)

Conversation outside the bathroom:

Jacob: Hey, baby, let's steal those little vodka bottles they have and get buzzed.
Keira: No, Jacob. Stop it. I don't want to.

(One of them slammed up against the flimsy bathroom door at that point. I had to pull my hat over my eyes because I was imagining Jacob kissing Keira all crazy against the bathroom door. There was the weakest of barriers between their love and me. I could hardly take it. I nearly passed out. I started counting by twos to chill out.)

Jacob: What? What do you mean?
Keira: I don't like when you drink. I know I was just around you that one time you drank too much, but it was icky. You're a mean drunk, Jacob. I hate saying that because I love you, but, dude, it's true.
Jacob: What? What are you talking about?
Keira: James's holiday party. You guys snuck liquor and thought you were so funny, but you were actually lame. You said mean crap to people. You told Sara she had a face only her mother could love or something like that. She cried, Jacob.
Jacob: God, I don't even remember that. You didn't say anything.
Keira: I know. It didn't come up again, so I was, like, well, maybe it was just a one-time deal. So look. No drinking right now. You can kiss me and do that thing you do with my hair and then let's sit back down. I gotta see what's up with Sara. I'm worried about her.
Jacob: I'm sorry, sweetness. You win.

And then I heard them kiss and make soft moaning sounds, and then I prayed that I'd die right there in the airplane bathroom, which is exactly the necessary dimensions for my coffin. My hips felt all smashed against the cold stainless steel, and my heart was crushed under the weight of their cruel perfect love.

And then I had to leave the bathroom because my safe zone had morphed into a torture chamber.

Now the flight attendants are bringing Sara to the back of the plane and doing something to her. I don't know. A bunch of the kids are out of their seats trying to figure out what is going on. James and John are tossing a football across the aisle as if they don't have a care in the world. Keira yelled at them: "Dudes—what the hell?" and they actually listened to her and stopped. John is clearly not the best boyfriend to have.

This just came over the loudspeaker: "Hello, passengers, this is the captain speaking. We are having a medical emergency that is going to require that we land the plane in Toronto, Canada. I sincerely apologize for this inconvenience. We are going to do our best to arrange connecting flights for all of you to get to your destination in a timely manner."

CANADA JOURNAL 3/2
#1 Entry from a hotel room in Toronto

We are in a hotel that hasn't had an upgrade for a thousand years. Everything is turquoise and orange and sticky and peeling. This place and the whole flight experience made me so anxious that I had to lock myself in the bathroom with the three hats I packed (furry black, green sherpa, and black beret) while I ritualistically put them on and then took them off my head while humming The Romantic Era's entire album. When people pounded on the door, which made me have to hum louder, I ignored them.

The second chaperone on the trip, Ms. Finley (Nurse Ratched), came by to give us a lecture on compliance. I was expecting her to tranquilize all of us because she said her nerves were shot and our activity level must "cease and desist."

James made John be a lookout at the front of the hall so kids could keep changing rooms at will. Eventually, everyone got hungry and they asked me to go buy Doritos, Lay's, Reese's Pieces, and popcorn at the mini-mart attached to the gas station next to the hotel. Mini-marts give me the total heebie-jeebies, but I couldn't let the entire class down, so I had to muster the strength to go by putting on my green sherpa and matching green Chucks. When I got there, I stood at the door, closed my eyes, counted to ten, took six deep breaths, clapped my hands twice, and then went in. I guess what happened to me in there was my reward from God or whoever exists to design these things on our behalf.

While I was in there, some Torontonian (or is it Toronitian or maybe Torontoino) male teenager actually looked at me like I was worth looking at and then talked to me. Stop it. I spoke back to him. Stop it again.

Here's the most unbelievable thing in the whole world aside from how delicious and *intoxicating* Jacob Kingston smells: this guy, his name is Brian, and he's a little fat, but who cares because I'm a lot fat, asked me for my room number. His dad works at the hotel, so he's there all the time. Get this—I gave him my room number. He'll probably never call me, but still, this is a major step in a direction that leads to people not thinking I'm a total freak.

CANADA JOURNAL 3/2
#2 Entry from a hotel room in Toronto, room 206, to be exact

(Jesus, he visits me.)

Sara's sickness is by far the best thing that has ever happened to me. It's been four hours since we checked into this hotel, and I bought snacks and met Brian. Ms. Finley has appeared once to tell us to stay in our rooms and that we have no definitive report on how Sara is doing.

At about the two-hour point, Brian knocked on my door and Keira answered. He had put on a nice collared shirt and was obviously nervous because I saw a little sweat around his short curly brown hair. When Keira realized the deal, she turned to me with big eyes and a wide-opened smile and said, "Well, Danielle, you work fast." She was being über-sweet when I know inside she was shocked that I had a "gentleman caller," as my mom would say.

He came in the room and all three of us just stared at one another for a while. Keira finally said, "Danielle, why don't you offer Brian some of the snacks you bought and you can, like, ask him about his school."

It got easier from there. We ate Reese's Pieces and he talked about being a senior in high school and other stuff, but I drifted off because I was in shock over my good fortune and then Jacob came over to our room to see Keira. He sported a stunned look on his face when he saw that there was a random guy in our room to see me.

Other people started coming into the room because Keira and Jacob were in there. A couple of times I saw Brian look over at me in a way that was, well, just so incredible. I mean it was like he liked me, maybe.

Brian had to go do something for his dad, but he grabbed my hand, squeezed it, and said he'd be back in a little bit. I had to write this all down. OMG!

✴CANADA JOURNAL✴ 3/2
#3 Entry: Nothing, ever, works out for me

I can't wait to leave this stupid hotel. The front desk dude confiscated the skateboard that James found outside the hotel and that he was riding in the hall. Brian came back as that was happening, and he stole the skateboard back from behind the desk. That made everyone think he was awesome.

One of the girls thought it would be fun if we played truth or dare. I had never done this ever but I knew kids did, and I knew the point of it. Everybody decided we would play, and no one kicked me out or anything, so I was included. James got chosen first and I wasn't even paying attention because I was lost in my own mind thinking about how amazing it was that a boy I could maybe kinda like (maybe even instead of Jacob) was in a hotel room with me. I was jolted back to reality after I must have unconsciously uttered "dare" when my turn came.

Keira said, "I dare you to kiss that guy you brought in here." Keira lifted her shoulders up to her ears and gave this tight-lipped smile, and the whole gesture said, "I'm helping ya, girl."

My heart totally pounded. I had never kissed someone. I didn't have any idea how to do it. But Brian got this look on his face that let me know he was willing to try. The whole room got silent because I know that they know that things this big and wonderful don't just happen to me. Even though it was kind of weird to be kissed in a gross hotel room in front of a group of kids who don't like me, I was still shaking with excitement.

A big part of me wanted everyone to see that I could be kissed. That I had lips on my face not just to bite when I was nervous and to eat too much with or to speak with occasionally. I, too, had lips on my face that could be kissed. I wanted them to see that. And they did. I don't think I was very good at it or that it was an earth-shattering, Mr. Darcy/Elizabeth-on-the-windy-heath-at-the-end-of-the-book kiss, but it was my kiss in the musty, dirty, paint-peeling, broken-down hotel room that was a metaphor for my life. It suited me. I was fine with it.

Brian moved slowly toward my face, and as he did everyone else receded into the background. For once, everyone else was in the background of my life instead of me being a pathetic extra in theirs. For this brief moment, I got to star in the scene. It would have been more exciting, I'm sure, if I were a more filmic player, but some things can't be helped.

Brian kissed me softly, the way I imagined a kiss should be from a boy. He didn't stay long, but it was long enough for me to feel warm and safe. I closed my eyes after he finished and hoped he liked it, too. My heart was racing as the game continued, but I didn't let that show on my face and I didn't talk. My voice would have come out in short, breathy stops that would *belie* the facade of calm I was desperately trying to construct.

Again, my mind drifted off somewhere until Heather drinking water from the toilet brought me back to the game. After Heather, it was Jacob's turn. She asked him "truth or dare?" Jacob, of course, chose "dare."

Heather said, "J-man, here's your dare: feel up Danielle outside her shirt."

"Heather!" Keira said as she looked over at me.

"What? You're worried your man will leave you for good after this? Hard-ly."

Keira just stared at her, and Jacob shrugged it off and gave Keira a quick hug.

There was a general snicker to set the stage for the event. There was a specific chill that ran down my spine. Jacob won't do this, I insisted inside myself.

"Remember, you don't do this and you have to drink toilet water."

"I know the rules, Heather," Jacob said as he got up from where he was sitting. He looked at me directly. To apologize for what was coming? To warn me? I don't know. Keira looked down slightly and held her hands in her lap. Jacob walked over to me and knelt down almost as if to pray. He didn't look at me. He looked away to his right. But he did it. He reached his hands out and put them over the T-shirt I was wearing, and which I will never wear again because I burned it in a lawless act outside the hotel room after this happened. He grabbed me where the dare insisted that he grab. It wasn't sexy. It wasn't warm. It was creepy and gross and everything terrible in one small gesture.

Brian got up and said, "Well, shit." And then he left. He obviously didn't know I was the chicken with blood on me in the henhouse. He didn't know when he saw me in the mini-mart that I was the butt of all jokes in this class, the least likely to be intimate with anyone, but he knew now and when that truth was made abundantly clear, he took off. I'll never see him again. Fine. I don't want to.

The game got broken up at that point because a lady from the hotel came in and said we were making too much noise. You couldn't break up the party five minutes before, lady?

Some people have so much. Some have so little. That game encapsulated both truths for me. The kiss from Brian was so much, my cup runneth over. Getting felt up by Jacob and having everyone giggle at the absurdity was throwing that full cup against the wall.

My mom had called and left a message while we were playing truth or dare. She and Dad were worried about me since they heard from the school that the plane had to land. They wanted me to call.

I love my parents, and I super hate that I need to write this here, but it is so hard to have parents that are so perfect. I feel like I throw what could have been a great life for them way off balance. It just sucks that the kid they have doesn't match the people they are.

I wanted to call them and say, "Hey, nothing much but the usual going on. We landed the plane in Canada because Sara got sick. The boy I'm hopelessly in love with felt me up in front of most of the class on a dare. Don't worry, it wasn't sexy. It won't be a notch on my lipstick case or anything. He pretty much had to do it or else he'd have to drink toilet water. Oh, I did kiss a boy I picked up in the mini-mart. How's it all with you?" But then they would want me to "talk through it all" and "be honest" with them, and that was just too impossible. I needed to be a private mess for the moment, a secret stain on the carpet. I couldn't handle them trying to clean me up. I ignored the call.

#4 Entry: Response to terrible truth-or-dare experience

I left the hotel room to get away from everyone and because I just couldn't write in my journal in front of Keira.

I started thinking about the book *A Separate Peace*. In it, Gene jostles the branch of a tree that his friend Phinney was standing on. Phinney falls off and, after a time, he actually dies from complications of that fall. It took place during World War II when some countries decided to find a separate peace from all the fighting. Gene, who was battling a different kind of war, a private psychological one because of his guilt, had to learn how to find a separate peace, too.

I am just like Gene.

The problem is that I like the idea of a separate peace, that it could exist and all, but I don't know how you get there. How do you get that peace when you just don't feel one ounce of peace at all?

I wish there was a pill I could take to keep me on life's straight path or a rope that could fall from the sky and once I grabbed it, I could be pulled to safety.

JOURNAL FROM A PLANE 3/4
#2 Airborne journal

Have no idea what landmass we are currently
flying over

Completely emotionally spent

(Need to hate Jacob)

Eventually, Ms. Harrison came back and told us that Sara's mom arrived and is staying with her in the hospital while she recovers. She's going to be fine! Thank God my toxic cloud of hate didn't do permanent damage to her.

What kind of person believes she emanates toxic vibes? A weird one.

I want to be normal. I want that thing to have never happened. I want Emily to come back. Stop writing on this topic, Danielle.

Instead, I am going to focus this journal on a way to hate Jacob Kingston, which is clearly what I need to do as a rational, functional human being. I must get practical about this. No person should love a boy who feels her up outside her shirt in front of her entire class on a stupid dare. No one should, but right now I still do. For some reason, right now, I still like him, even though he made me sad beyond words, and I snuck off several times in the airport to go into a bathroom stall and cry because I just had to. I don't know how much the crying helped because I still love Jacob. Now I am going to start trying to not love him. Ten reasons to not love Jacob:

He loves Keira.

He felt me up on a dare with no emotion whatsoever, like it was no big deal.

He doesn't always brush his hair. (I actually like that.)

He has terrible handwriting. (Arg, who cares?)

He sags his pants, which I know is in style but I hate it. (But it actually looks good on him.)

He doesn't really talk to me.

He doesn't really even know I exist even after he felt me up on a stupid dare.

He acts like that dare never happened.

He eats sandwiches on white bread.

He's an asshole.

I might get somewhere with #10. I just need to *embellish* somewhat, flesh it out, but I think I can go somewhere with this.

Arrrrg, of all the damn moments to get writer's block.

He's totally an asshole and I totally love him.

I'm an idiot.

CLASS ASSIGNMENT 3/5
Journal #1 of the England Trip

(Covering day one of the trip. Ms. Harrison likes my take on the day. A)

Danielle Levine
English 12
Ms. Harrison
Period 4

Ms. Harrison, I am über-happy that you got all of us (well, sans one) to England in one piece. That was quite an experience, which I will remember for the rest of my life. Not many people can say they have been on a plane when it had to land midflight because some kid got sick. Well, this is probably not what you want to read in my journal, as I am sure living the experience was enough for you. From here on out, I will do my best to recount the most memorable parts of the trip for you as instructed.

I think you'll remember that the first day started with a trip to Knightsbridge, where I peered in the windows at Harry Nichols and Burberry. Gosh, to be the kind of person who could buy those things. I am not, so I will just move on and attempt to live presently, in the now, instead of wishing. That is something my yoga teacher, David, talks a lot about. He says breathing can only happen in the present. So if you are stressed or worried about the past or the future, you can stop and focus on your breath, which is with you right NOW. You might want to try that given how stressful it is to deal with us. I am, right now, on this very trip, this very second, trying desperately to live in the NOW so that various other things from the PAST exit my brain permanently. Sorry, you probably don't need to know about that.

Anyway, after that we drove past the Wellington Arch and on to Buckingham Palace. Outside the palace, there were all these poor guard-type people with huge black hats and red outfits, and they had to stand super-still and not even really acknowledge us. I would be so annoyed with that job, and I would need to up my Adderall dosage for sure.

After that we went to the Theatre Royal on Drury Lane. This theatre was around for 340 years, and it had 1,662 bricks in the building. I was so happy to hear that because I was so tired from jet lag by the time we got to the building that if the tour guide woman, who was dressed in that Restoration-drama outfit, had given out any specific numbers about the building that weren't even numbers, my OCD would have kicked into overdrive and you might have had to take me to the hospital— LOL—not really, but I might have panicked a little. I just like when numbers are even that's all.

Next, we saw street performers in Trafalgar Square. I liked that better than the palace because I saw a juggler. A little weird, right? But, in spite of myself and my mood at the time, this guy made me smile. This man just stood there and juggled.

A lot of chaos and noise and shenanigans and stuff were going on right around him and none of it seemed to bother him. A double-decker tour bus spewed a black cloud of exhaust right in his face and he just kept on smiling and juggling, throwing balls in the air like that was what he was meant to do. He calmed me down and I felt something that might actually be described as peace. Amazing, right?

Teacher comments: *Nice job recounting the day. Thanks for reminding me to breathe.*

PRIVATE TRIP INFO 3/5
Journal #1: The real story

The hotel where we stayed was under construction, and scaffolding was set up outside each of our rooms. Jacob came running into Keira's and my room, flung our window open, and said, "Ladies, look out here—our own private nightclub." I leaned out the window with Keira, and we saw all our classmates running around, hanging out, dancing and laughing. James and John were already climbing down the scaffolding on their way to roam free in this foreign city. Jacob yelled down at them, "Hey, J & J, wait up. Let me change and I'll be right down." He leaned in to Keira and kissed her and then pulled off his T-shirt. For a glorious never-to-be-repeated second, he stood there bare chested. Jesus. Pause for my jaw to drop.

Jacob ran to his room and Keira followed him, although she

took a second and looked back at me. She hasn't said much to me since her boyfriend felt me up. It's kinda awkward for her, too, I guess. Then there was a bustling outside my room as the kids who weren't already on the scaffolding gathered to get going. Keira said, "Hey, Danielle, come with us. The teachers are asleep; we won't get caught."

"No, Keira, it's all right. I'm going to stay here."

It's late as I write this, and, pretty quickly after they all left, the hotel floor quieted to a heavy silence. The strangest thought hit me: I don't like Sara, it's true, but I feel her missing from the group.

A soul-size portion of regret rose in my throat. It's doing a number on my gut right now.

A part of me wishes so much that I could be bad with them, that I could join the rebel spirit and go exploring in the night just like they were. I am still so envious of all of them. So jealous of their crazy, blind courage because there was a time when I was just like them, but that version of me is gone. The new version, Danielle 2.0, has a lot of design flaws.

I sat on the floor beneath the open window while the cold night air blew the white curtains above me like giant surrender flags.

I pulled my black furry hat down over my face and wrapped my arms around my bent knees, pulling them as tightly to my chest as I could and then I cried.

David would tell me to just sit with this pain, embrace it, live in it, and then something new, by virtue of the miracle of life in the present, would enter. That's such a nutty idea. But what else have I got going on tonight. I have no idea how to work the television that's in our room so my pain just might be the only show in town for the evening.

CLASS ASSIGNMENT 3/6
Journal #2 of the England Trip

(Covering days 2-4 of the trip. I get another A.
Perhaps travel writing is my niche.)

Danielle Levine
English 12
Ms. Harrison
Period 4

Over the last few days, as you know, Ms. Harrison, we took long bus rides to places such as Warwick Castle. Boy, were those bus rides long. You may want to reconsider the itinerary to exclude long bus rides. I'm just saying that it can be hard for kids to stay calm and stuff, and they might misbehave while you are sleeping.

Warwick Castle was really something. We learned about ingeniously cruel ways people were tortured in the past. The tour guide said that people used to have boiling sand poured inside their armor; it often burned people alive. Even without modern technology, people were cruel. How do you like that? Made me feel kinda hopeless that we haven't progressed much.

Anyway, moving on . . .

After Warwick Castle we went to Stratford-upon-Avon, which I just love, and got a tour from a petite woman with a charming British accent who carried a very long plastic daisy (three feet long, at least) in her hand so we wouldn't lose her. I thought it was cute and incredibly helpful for someone like me who benefits from a homing device. We toured Shakespeare's school and house and grave. His bedroom and bed were so small I couldn't help but think about how little people were in the past. If I lived in Stratford-upon-Avon during Shakespeare's time, they probably would have burned me for a witch or mistook me for a cow and chopped me up and served me for dinner. Aside from terrible recurring thoughts about how fat I am, I had a good day in Stratford.

The next day we visited Oxford, and all I remember from that old city is that it was infested with rats. I couldn't hear anything after the tour guide mentioned the Black Death and all the rats. I have to stop writing about that right now. Next we visited Stonehenge—much better.

Surprisingly, this bunch of big rocks helped me be able to let go of some things I won't go into here specifically, but, I thought, if something like Stonehenge can exist and the greatest minds of our times can't figure it out, then maybe all the things about my life that I can't make sense out of aren't to be unraveled. Maybe some things are meant to be a mystery.

That idea doesn't solve anything, but it does make me stop and let go, just briefly. I am by no means capable of *extrapolating* all the meaning from my life situation. Certain things are just there like big, giant otherworldly stones that appeared somehow, obviously, but not by any rational means. What can you do? You can't bring people back from the dead. You can't make people love you. You can't really force much at all. All you can do is just be. (Although, face it, that is easier said than done.) It would be cool, though, if something about me made someone stare in wonder like I stared at Stonehenge. That would be cool indeed.

Teacher comments: *Aside from your thoughts about yourself in Stratford, this trip is giving you good perspective.*

POSTCARD #1 to Aunt Joyce

Dear Aunt Joyce,

I am sure you know by now, because it wasn't on the news, but I did not die in a plane crash on the way to London. Things are manageable, I guess, so far.

Danielle

Journal #2: The real story

On the bus ride out of London to Warwick Castle, Heather and James and Michelle and John played a game called nervous. What is this game? I asked myself when I heard James say they should play it. This is a game you play with someone you like, someone you would love to have touch you. If heaven were a fantasy I could live out, I'd play nervous with Jacob for eternity. But I would not, in no uncertain terms, make it a spectator sport. Just stop it, Danielle. Jacob is a jerk. This cognitive dissonance over him is going to make me need immediate psychiatric care. So, in nervous, one member of the couple (in the case of our bus ride, the guy) starts touching the other person in various places on her body or starts trying to kiss her or make progressively bold, amorous gestures until the girl says "nervous" and then the boy has to pull back or stop or whatever. I could never actually play this game. If a guy just so much as put his hand on my overgrown thigh I'd yell "nervous!" at a decibel sure to break the sound barrier.

The teachers were asleep at the front of the bus and the driver wore headphones and was completely not interested in any of us or what we were doing. John played this game with Michelle, and I wanted to say aloud, "Hey, excuse me, guys, but Michelle is NOT his girlfriend. Isn't anyone going to stand up for Sara here?" But what do I know? I don't know the rules of love. John was actually being really gentle as he brushed his hand along Michelle's ankle, and she turned red and giggled a little. She didn't utter "nervous." She didn't look nervous, either. She glowed.

James was trying to play nervous with Heather. You could tell by how committed to the game he was that he was all about touching her. But Heather couldn't focus because she was talking to Keira.

"Keira, I don't know if you'd be cool with this, but for tonight could I sleep in your room? Michelle and I got into a fight because she thinks I took her leggings, which I so didn't. The ones I'm wearing are mine. Anyway, can I?"

"I don't care. I guess. Danielle, do you care if Heather sleeps with us tonight?"

OMG I totally do! But instead I say, "No."

"Awesome. Keira, do you have a razor? I forgot mine and my bikini line is totally out of control." Heather said that out loud on the bus. Appalling.

And then the rest of the bus ride I was trapped between watching couples engage in nervous and listening to Heather talk about shaving her lady parts. I thought that was going to be as bad as it got, but, no, when we got back to the hotel I had to watch Heather straddle the toilet and trim her pubic hair with Keira's razor. I think I stared at her like she was a mutant species. She took it in stride, though.

"You wanna use this razor when I'm done, Danielle?"

"No, I'm good. Thanks."

I am having a hard time finding common ground with any of these people.

POSTCARD #2 to Aunt Joyce

Dear Aunt Joyce,
   I am learning a lot more than just stuff about England. I will fill you in when I get back because I don't want random mail people reading the personal junk about my life.
   Love you,
   Danielle

CLASS ASSIGNMENT 3/7
Journal #3 of the England Trip

(Covering day 5 of the trip. I have a lot to say to
Ms. Harrison. A.)

Danielle Levine
English 12
Ms. Harrison
Period 4

Today began with a visit to Westminster Abbey, which is a place I just love. It's beautiful. Famous writers are buried there, and I love to stand in the writers' corner and soak in the intelligence buried there. You can feel it.

You know what? I can't focus on writing about the Abbey and the other stuff we did today, because, well, I just have to get something off my chest. I want to tell you the truth about something embarrassing that I did. You are my teacher, and I think you are a pretty smart lady about facts and stuff and also about feelings. So I am going to risk being honest here and just hope it falls on the compassionate ears I think you have.

I know I fell behind when we visited Big Ben and, because I didn't stay with the group, I wasn't with everyone when you did a head count on Downing Street. I know you were mad, and you had a right to be. Your job on this trip is hard and we shouldn't make it harder. I just want to tell you why I fell behind. You can still be mad, but maybe you'll understand a little.

By the time we got to Big Ben after taking the boat ride on the Thames, seeing the Crown Jewels, and watching the boys do handstands on the Tower Bridge, the sun was starting to set. It was very beautiful to me. The sky was gray, but streaks of orange offset it and I just kept staring, and I got lost in that staring instead of listening to the tour guide. When my eyes came back to earth, they fell on a young couple standing in front of the clock. Maybe you saw them. He was wearing tight black jeans with a sweatshirt, his hood down to reveal thick black hair to his shoulders. A chain dangled over his jeans pocket and his shoelaces were untied. He was cute, Ms. Harrison, he really was. His cuteness wasn't all about his looks, either. It was very much about what he was doing and the way he was doing it, standing next to Big Ben.

He was with his girlfriend (well, I guessed she was his girlfriend), and he was kissing the life out of her. (I really hope it is okay that I am writing this to you. I really want to.) He was giving her one of those kisses that you see in movies or read about in books, where I pretty much think the whole rest of the world disappeared for him, even the majesty of that big clock behind him. And, see, that was part of what really mesmerized me. He was having a timeless moment under the biggest symbol of time on the planet. (As an English teacher, I am sure you already thought of that irony as you read this before I even mentioned it, but still I wanted to tell you that I got it.)

His girlfriend looked just like Juno, except she wasn't pregnant. Well, truthfully, I couldn't really know that. Maybe she was and that's why they were kissing the way I saw. I am sure making a baby together can inspire that kind of kissing. But she wasn't visibly pregnant is what I'm saying. She was just really, really cute and smart looking with short dark hair and tiny thighs like Juno, like a British Juno because she was pretty pale, and I really have no idea about her teeth.

Anyway, like I said before, her boyfriend was kissing the life out of her, or the soul out of her, something was being kissed out of her. I saw her rise up on her toes from the power of his kiss. She was so moved by this kiss that she just dropped her bag to the ground, probably not caring if someone walked off with all her possessions because someone was loving her so passionately in that moment that all her things meant nothing.

Ms. Harrison, I am sure a scene like this is familiar to you. I am sure someone has kissed you like that. Maybe not under Big Ben, but maybe the Empire State Building or something (LOL). The point is, no one has ever kissed me like that and watching those two, I thought about how it is truly possible that no one ever will. Please, please, please just let me write this to you without you giving my words to Marv or my mom. Please. I don't think this is psychotic. I think it is truly just honest and that is not *pathological.*

So I stared at them and I watched this boy *ravenously* kiss this girl. It was incredible. Like he was malnourished and eating from a delicious buffet that was about to pack up for the night. And he needed to get as much as he could before it was taken away. And she . . . well, you know that line from Hamlet's first soliloquy about the way Gertrude loved Hamlet's father: "Why, she would hang on him, as if increase of appetite had grown by what it fed on." It was just like that. They were both increasingly hungry for the buffet that was each other. (I won't extend this metaphor anymore. I think you get my point.) But it just stunned me, stunned me and made me lose the moment we were in as a class. I didn't see or feel you all move and get on the bus. I just didn't know you did that.

I am sorry I got left behind, and I am sorry I caused a hassle for you when you counted everyone and I wasn't there. I just wanted you to know that I was lost from the group because, well, I am truly lost from the group. I am sorry, Ms. Harrison.

Teacher comments: *It's okay, Danielle. We've all moved on from that moment. You can forgive yourself.*

POSTCARD #1 to Mom and Dad

Dear Mom and Dad,

Everything is fine. England is as lovely as it always is. Thanks for sending me on the trip.

Love you,
Danielle

POSTCARD #3 to Aunt Joyce

Dear Aunt Joyce,
   I know you will probably get this postcard after I get home, but I am sending it because I want to remember to ask you if you've ever been kissed really passionately in a place that was the perfect background for such a momentous event and what that was like. To the mail people who may be reading this postcard: you are perverts who shouldn't be spending work hours reading other people's mail.

   Love you,
   Danielle

PRIVATE TRIP INFO 3/7
Journal #3: The real story

   Heather called me a bitch to my face because room check was earlier tonight because I held up the bus. I literally tried biting the inside of my cheek like girls do in television movies in order not to cry. It didn't work. It just gave me another reason to want to cry.
   I stayed in the room and pretended I was invisible.
   I know this wish to be invisible is ironic since I am twenty pounds overweight. I mean, if I were truly committed to this

invisibility thing I should have developed anorexia, but I am not that lucky.

People may not see me or they may ignore me as I desire them to, but the force of life does not ignore me. It just keeps acting upon me in the most impersonal way like gravity. There is something profound, I'm sure, to be learned from this, but I can't possibly find my way to that right now. What I am going to find my way to is the phone so I can order room service.

CLASS ASSIGNMENT 3/8
Journal #4 of the England Trip

(Covering day 6 of the trip. A.)

Danielle Levine
English 12
Ms. Harrison
Period 4

Today we went on a walking tour of Canterbury, an incredible city. Is it a city? Or a village? Or maybe it's a *hamlet*? Anyway, whatever Canterbury is, I like it. Our tour guide was an old woman who told us she was born in Canterbury and had lived there her whole life and couldn't imagine living anywhere else. In fact, she said she plans to haunt the place after she dies (LOL).

She was married once, she said, in another lifetime when she was very young, but her husband died when he fell off a scaffolding as he was refurbishing one of the churches in their neighborhood. If anyone gets to go to heaven, she said, it must be her husband, Bubbles, (that's so cute) because he died in the service of the Lord even though he spent his weekends at the pub. Some things you do make the Lord turn a blind eye to some other things, she told us. She's a relativist, she said, and while I am still trying to figure out exactly what that means, I know I want to be a relativist, too.

Ms. Harrison, I am going to write about the stuff we saw in Canterbury, but I have to write about this woman first because she is what I will most remember about my visit to Canterbury and probably what I will most remember about my whole trip to England, along with some other small details that I won't write about here.

Justine (that was our guide's name in case you don't remember) started out our walking tour by giving each of us a piece of candy because she said young people can pay attention better if they have something to do with their mouths other than talk. Also, a little something sweet never hurt anybody. Her mother named her Justine eighty years ago on the day she was born, and she liked the name just fine until she read *Frankenstein* and that was the name of the innocent young girl who was falsely accused and hanged for killing the young Frankenstein boy. It took her some time to come to terms with her name after that, but she came to realize there was a lot about life that you just had to come to terms with, and she hoped we would learn that lesson sooner rather than later.

Which brought us to the entrance of the Canterbury Cathedral and Justine's lecture about how, whether we liked it or not, we had to come to terms with the Starbucks that was situated right at the entrance. Christianity was established in Canterbury in the year six hundred she said, and Starbucks was established in two thousand, and those were just two facts we would have to come to terms with. The Cathedral and the Coffeehouse (she said both should be capitalized) were places of worship to two similar and yet different gods. She didn't elaborate and I will have to think about that more, but I am sure she is right.

Justine is the most wrinkled woman I have ever seen. And I have to tell you this, Ms. Harrison: I really thought she was beautiful. I can't believe I thought that, but I did. Usually, when I think of old people I get kind of sad. I think how awful it must be to be so old. But I had a real *epiphany* as I listened to and watched Justine. Sometimes it is awful to be young, so where was I getting the idea that it was so much worse to be old?

After the tour of the Cathedral, you gave us free time for lunch. Everyone paired off and went their separate ways, and I was left standing at the front of the Cathedral thinking it was fine, that I would have lunch by myself in this beautiful place. But then, Justine asked if I wanted to have lunch with her. I did. I said yes. I was both surprised and happy with myself for that decision.

Instead of going to a restaurant, Justine took me back to her flat (that's what she called her little apartment), and she served us authentic shepherd's pie she had made herself. I really liked it because it tasted so good and was served in these small antique-looking ceramic pie pans. I had never eaten anything so cute!

Her home, which was on the second floor above a repair shop, looked just like something out of a storybook: everything was old and creaky and a little dusty. There was not one thing (not even a fork or knife) that looked like it came from Ikea or Target or Restoration Hardware. She didn't really have a color scheme or design of any kind; it was very *eclectic*. She had old books stacked on every shelf and piled in every corner. Pieces of yellowed paper with wise quotes hung on her refrigerator by magnets. Pictures and paintings in old frames covered all her walls. I could have spent weeks there asking her about all the pictures and the quotes, but if I had done that I really would have missed the bus again! I just asked her about one picture. It hung to the left of the window that looked out onto the street and right above her dining table, which seated two. It was an old black-and-white photo of a man in a suit and tie with perfectly trimmed hair. He had very kind eyes. "Is that your husband?" I asked.

"It was."

And then she told me all about Bubbles. About how he wouldn't serve in the army even though I guess he was supposed to. How he said he would only put on a uniform that made him truly be of service to humanity, which is why he worked in restoration. Justine said she was so proud of what Bubbles did for a living. He spent a lot of time restoring the tile work in the old buildings in Canterbury. It was very tedious, specific work meant only for artists who had a sense of history and who cared about future generations in a very real sense. "Little things, little things, are much more important than big things. Big things hit you in the face with their bigness and obscure the little, more important things that really define a life and provide it with delicacy." I've quoted her here because I remember, *verbatim* what she said because it sounded so real and so true. I wished I understood it the same way her face showed that she did.

I must have looked a little confused so she said politicians and movie stars and bank accounts were big things that got in the way of living. And when I said to her that, well, you need a bank account to survive, she said I was dead wrong. She said it just like that—*dead wrong*. Then she pulled out a glass milk bottle that had lots of cash shoved in it. "This is my bank account and it works just fine, thank you very much." I wanted to ask her a million questions about how she lived like that and didn't she feel like she was missing out or wasn't she worried someone would break in and steal her money. She didn't get to travel or buy new things, but I kind of knew the answer she would have given. Her small life made her happy. Her special life was all she needed.

Ms. Harrison, Justine never had one bit of plastic surgery

her whole life. I didn't ask her that, but I just know it's true. I mean, if you're a woman who keeps all your money in a glass milk bottle, then you don't have the resources or the inclination for plastic surgery. She was eighty years old with so many wrinkles, even on places that I didn't know you could get wrinkles, like on her forearms. Each one fascinated me. She reminded me so much of the lead actress in *Harold and Maude*. Have you seen that movie? If you haven't you really should. You'd like it. Anyway, Justine had that same spirit of acceptance, that same adorableness that Ruth Gordon possessed. We are wrong if we think old people are freaky and pathetic. Well, I guess some of them can be. Just like some young people can be freaky and pathetic.

At the end of lunch, before we walked back to meet the group, Justine wrote down her address and said we could be pen pals. She said she had been wanting to write letters to someone in another country and thought I would do just fine, thank you very much.

After my lunch with Justine, we saw the Christopher Marlowe theatre, and we learned about how Canterbury got a new archbishop in 2003. When I read the *Canterbury Tales* again at some point in my life, I will have a whole new set of pictures in my head about the setting of those stories.

For my room at home, I was able to find a snow globe featuring the Canterbury Cathedral and some postcards of cobblestone alleys. When I look at them in the future, they'll remind me of Justine.

I guess for you, the most dramatic part of the day was when James came back from lunch with a giant tattoo of the British flag on his left pectoral. Well, maybe even more dramatic was when we got back to the hotel, and it was clear from his fever that the tattoo was infected. Looked like maybe you had a fever, too, because you were boiling mad. LOL. Hope it's not too soon to joke about this.

Teacher comments: *What a rich experience with history and humanity you had. Thanks for sharing!*

PRIVATE TRIP INFO 3/8
Journal #4: The real story

I am happy to report that tonight I don't really need a private journal because my day was so wonderful, and I already wrote all the details to Ms. Harrison. I had nothing to hide. Awesome.

CLASS ASSIGNMENT 3/9
Journal #5 of the England Trip

(Covering the last day of the trip. Another A. I am on
a roll.)

Danielle Levine
English 12
Ms. Harrison
Period 4

Well, this was our last day in England. We started with a visit to the Tate Modern Museum. I am so happy you included that museum on our tour, Ms. Harrison. Thank you. I lost myself in the photography exhibit section, unbelievably, but Keira personally invited me to check it out with her, and I did. I saw how some photographs make a positive statement.

My favorite piece was pictures of a woman who chronicled her journey of losing ten pounds. She took a picture of herself naked every day from her starting point of 140 pounds to her ending point of 130 pounds. If you looked at each picture in succession you didn't notice much change. But if you stepped back and looked at the first picture and then the last, you could see how different she looked.

Our lives are like that. We all probably change a little every day and we don't really notice the changes. But if we look at ourselves today and think back to a year ago, we might be surprised by what we find. It's hard to bring change into our lives, I think, and so that's why it doesn't really happen radically most of the time. Although, wait, sometimes things do change radically without our choice. I guess what I am talking about is conscious change. That kind of change I think takes time like the diet woman showed through her photographs.

Anyway, that's just one example of what is so cool about the Tate. Also, that exhibit made me want to go on a diet (but not photograph myself along the way. LOL).

After the Tate, we did the Southwark Riverside Walk, and I got to have a good conversation with a classmate. (You're probably surprised, but it's true and maybe now I won't have to see Marv anymore because I am learning to socialize.)

Then we got a tour of the Globe Theatre before we all rode the London Eye and got a spectacular view of the city where I took a moment to realize how small we really are in the scheme of things. And that reminded me of what Justine had said about the beauty of small things, that it's just fine that we have small lives; those are probably better.

Teacher comments: *Nice summation of a beautiful trip.*

(A very satisfying journal to write.)

I am still just amazed any time something good happens to me. But today was one of those days, and I will just admit that as I sit here and type this journal, I am still amazed. When we did the Southwark Riverside Walk I was walking at a slower pace than everyone else because I was soaking in every image I could before we left. I really do love London. Someday, perhaps, I can live there.

Anyway, I wasn't paying attention, and I tripped and fell right over Jacob. He fell, too. Everyone laughed but kept on walking and there we were, Jacob and I, on the ground. I expected him to say something like "Hey, watch out" or "What the hell are you doing?", but he didn't. Instead, I said something stupid. I said this: "You should have just drank the toilet water!" I don't know where the words came from. They just came out. All my complicated feelings for him came out in the line, "You should have just drank the toilet water!" And then I did something even worse. I started to cry. Luckily, the rest of the group kept walking, and miraculously, Jacob didn't walk away.

"What?" he said. I was some other being in that moment, someone who actually, I guess, had something to say.

"You should have drank the toilet water in that hotel room

in Canada instead of doing what you did." And then he looked at me while I cried for a little while longer.

When he spoke, his words appeared like a typed message across the clear tablet of my mind. I can see them now. He said, "Look, Danielle, why would I have drank the toilet water? Why would I do that? That would have been totally disgusting. It didn't even occur to me to drink that instead of touching you. I thought I was being as gentle as I possibly could, and I just touched you. There wasn't anything disgusting to me about that. I'm really sorry it pissed that guy off, but I thought he knew I didn't mean anything bad. I really, really didn't. I'm sorry, Danielle."

And then I tried really hard to speak again, but the me that had something to say just left. This was all I could get out: "I just . . . I just . . . it's just." And then Jacob saved me from myself right there.

"I don't know why you don't give yourself any credit. You are what you are, Danielle, and it's fine. It's cool. I mean no one in this class can wear hats like you do. It's cool."

I don't know, maybe in this case writing it down makes it lose some of its impact. I don't know if I can fully explain even to myself in words just how much better that all made me feel. But it did. I forgave him for feeling me up. I forgave myself for thinking he was trying to humiliate me. I don't know, I just stopped being angry about it, and even though it seems like just a small little thing . . . it felt like a big, awesome thing.

AUNT JOYCE E-MAIL 3/11
First E-mail (#1) from Aunt Joyce after
England trip

Sweet Danielle,

I have to hear everything about your trip! I am very interested
in who you are after that experience. We'll talk soon.

Your Forever Aunt Joyce

P.S. As for your question about whether or not I've been
kissed passionately in a picturesque setting, the answer is
yes. However, before you get too jealous or excited, I want
to point out that it was with Claude that guy I met in Paris
who was sexy and affectionate but who, I subsequently
learned, was only that way from taking Ecstasy. So, see, not
all fantasies are as great as you imagine.

JUSTINE LETTER 3/12
Letter #1 to Justine that I write when I get
back to California

Dear Justine,
    It's Danielle. Remember me? I am the redheaded
girl that you had over to your house for lunch when

you gave my class a tour of Canterbury. My lunch with you was one of my favorite parts of the whole trip. I really want to thank you for that. I'm not sure I properly thanked you when I was with you because I was just so awestruck by you, your home, and your life.

I remember everything you told me over lunch, and there was one thing that really stuck with me. You told me that Bubbles didn't join the army like he was supposed to, and that reminded me of a book I read, and I guess I just want to tell you about it. Maybe you'll want to read the book because I noticed you had a lot of books around your place. The book is called The Things They Carried, and it's by Tim O'Brien, who was a soldier in the Vietnam War. He struggled with his decision to go to Vietnam and he even thought about going to Canada, which many people would have considered cowardly at the time.

Tim O'Brien wrote in his book that "I survived, but it's not a happy ending. I was a coward. I went to war." (Sometimes I remember certain things perfectly and forever. Like those words, which I know were on page 61.) When you were talking about Bubbles, it made me think of that line because Bubbles did something that some people would call cowardly and other people would call brave. One decision, two totally different perspectives. Very baffling.

Well, I hope you are doing well in Canterbury and

enjoying the tours you are giving. I also hope you don't have to give too many tours to wild high school kids like us (LOL—that means laugh out loud).
    Sincerely,
    Danielle

MARV MISSIVE
Letter #1 from Marv to me after the school trip

Danielle,
    How was your trip and your spring break? How are you doing? Anything you'd like to discuss after that experience?
    Marv

MARV MISSIVE
Letter #1 from me to Marv after school trip written during lunch

(I get brave)

Marv,
    Have you ever been felt up by a boy you really liked on a dare? Have you ever known such pure humili-

ation and objectification? Pretend this question is for literary purposes only. How you respond will tell me a lot about you and determine whether or not I will ever trust you again. No pressure.

    Danielle

MARV MISSIVE
Letter #2 from Marv to me after the trip

Danielle,

    I have not experienced that particular brand of shame, but that does not mean I have avoided shame altogether. When I was in high school, I was deeply (and I mean deeply) in love with a woman who was quite a bit older than me and who cast a certain spell over me. She was, in every way, a goddess. In my mind, she still is. One day, I saw fit to tell her just how transfixed I was in her presence. I'll spare you all the details, but she literally laughed in my face. She was sure I was telling her these things on a childish dare. She threw a lamp at me and told me never to speak to her again. I didn't. Every time I was around her, I looked at the ground. To this day, I wince when I think about the incident. Frankly, it was difficult for me to write to you about it.

    Marv

MARV MISSIVE
Letter #2 from me to Marv after the trip

Marv,
   Then you understand that <u>Love</u> is one cruel bitch.
   Danielle

MARV MISSIVE
Letter #3 from Marv to me

Danielle,
   Yes, Danielle, indeed I do.
   Marv

MENTAL HEALTH MISSIVE 3/19
Letter #2 for the Commitment Hearing
Committee regarding my social skills class

Dear Commitment Hearing Committee (who I am sure I am appearing before because of the social skills class I was forced to attend by my therapist and parents. Please refer to first letter to you for more details regarding this <u>travesty</u>.)
   I had a week of what I would characterize as "semifun" with my peers in England, and then I had a

spring break where I rested and felt just shy of normal most of the time and where I completely forgot about the fact that I would have to attend a social skills class when I returned. Charles, Megan, Andy, and Iggie will, I'm sure, be committed to some maximum-security facility before I will, so perhaps the committee has met them already. They are a quartet of social mismanagement, and I just hate being named in any group with them.

Megan's mom comes to the class with her and sits until her daughter "gets acclimated." Megan wears very big sweaters and hides beneath them. If I had her body I would live forever in a nudist colony.

Andy and Charles ride the bus together to get here and show up covered in grease; they work on cars all day. They both have long hair that they let hang in front of their faces. I think so maybe Lisa can't see them. I gotta admire that move, I guess.

I can't make any sense out of Iggie whose chair was yet again littered with all the paper creatures he folds and rips and talks to during the two-hour nightmare that is this class. It is possible, however, that he is a savant and these paper thingies may be brilliant works of art.

Daniel is an island all to himself, and I don't think he'll end up committed like the rest of us, so I didn't mention his name at the beginning of this missive.

I'm not even sure why he needs to be here.

Today, Lisa made us discuss the differences between what we wish our lives were like and what they are currently like. I was irritated at the assumption that all of us wished our lives were different. (I'm sure we all do, but still, I hate that this woman, who I don't know, is so acutely aware of that pain in all of us.) I didn't say anything to her about my irritation but Daniel did. He said the question was "arrogant, pointed, and judgmental," that all of us had to "lay bare certain vulnerabilities that we, as a group, were not ready to do," and if Lisa had been doing this line of work for any substantive length of time, she would know that and he resented being an early case in her career. Honestly, Daniel rocks.

Lisa listened to Daniel but didn't change her line of questioning. She sat perfectly up in her too bright suit and continued, "Sooo, who would like to start . . . Danielle?"

I forced this response: "Everybody's life is a series of what is versus what we wish it was, isn't it? Is there anybody who has everything just the way they like it?"

But then she reminded me that we were taking this moment in time to talk about my particular life and so could I please be specific about mine.

Sigh and continue.

"I want to be twenty pounds lighter."

And then a whole lot of language came out of Lisa. Language about how that was a brave statement, how that is something that can be accomplished, goals can be set, and changes can be made incrementally . . . blah, blah, blah, blah, blah . . . I heard some of it but stopped listening until Daniel said, "Yeah, she can do all that and maybe feel better and be more social, but then there will be something after that. Like she won't like her hair color, which I really dig, by the way, or she'll want a whole new wardrobe. I mean the other response you could have given her was that she could consider that she's fine just the way she is, that everyone comes to this planet in a different package, and the one she has is pretty okay. That's what I would have said if I was wearing the russet suit and carrying the master's degree."

And then there was this whole exchange between Daniel and Lisa about how Daniel always chooses to be contrary and how that creates conflict in relationships and he may want to consider that there are other ways of looking at things than his way, and Daniel told her she should try swallowing some of the medicine she was doling out. It's really obvious that Lisa can't stand Daniel. I think Daniel may actually like Lisa in a strange way because she brings out this side of him that he enjoys. I don't know, that's just

127

my opinion. At one point, I turned and gave Daniel a smile as a way of thanking him for taking up my cause. He gave me a supportive nod.

After that, I kind of drifted off into another world so I didn't have to be in this one, in a church basement that smelled of old cigarettes and burned coffee, feeling lost among people who I know in my heart are brethren.

**#1 AUNT JOYCE JOURNAL* 3/24
My talk with her

Aunt Joyce came over to see me and talk to me about the trip. My whole family had dinner in the dining room where Joyce commented on Mom's cheery choice of yellow walls and the vase of red spring flowers she keeps on the table. Mom has style just like Aunt Joyce. After dinner, Aunt Joyce and I went up into my room so we could pull out the vintage clothes from the back of the closet and try stuff on.

I mainly just put on different hats while I talked about Justine, but Joyce was having fun stepping in and out of dresses.

Finally, she said, "Lady, give me the teenage dirt."

I gave her this very wide-eyed look and she read my mind.

"What happened? . . . Did you kiss someone?"

"How did you know? OMIGOD."

"Perimenopausal women have killer instincts. Spill it."

"Well, it wasn't all that. It was pretty much like The Romantic Era's lyric 'Your kiss is cold, my mind is numb.' Yeah, it ended up being exactly that but, whatever, at least I can say I've been kissed."

"Ah, life will never be the same."

"Well, it got worse from there. The guy I kissed took off when Jacob, the boy I'm in love with, felt me up. Jacob didn't want to feel me up; he had to or else he'd have to drink toilet water. So, there it is, my sex life in a nutshell."

Aunt Joyce laughed and got a few more details out of me and then said, "You know what, my sex life boils down to similar tales but with adult players. You're gonna be fine, kid. Just fine. Give it a little time for the bruises to heal. Oh, I almost forgot. Come with me to my car. I found two old parasols for us. Let's get them and walk about in the garden."

More than anyone I know, Aunt Joyce takes things that I think are *unmitigated* disasters and shrinks them down to manageable size.

MENTAL HEALTH MISSIVE 3/26
Letter #3 for the Commitment Hearing
Committee (So they know my fall into total
mental illness was the result of extenuating
circumstances set loose by adults who were
supposed to be helping me.)

Dear CHC,

Just to be clear, I am writing this letter during my
social skills class. I have been allowed to bring my
journal in here because Lisa has no idea what she's
doing and thinks each of us should be allowed "to
find pure expression in any context." (Whatever that
means.) Along with my journal, I brought four of my
hats, just in case I need them. Lisa keeps talking
about how spring has sprung and it is a time of
rebirth and renewal or whatever, and I just want to
keep writing to keep myself distracted so I miss most
of what she's saying.

Charles has brought his guitar, and I have to say
that it is so distracting to have him accent people's
talking with riffs. He's not very good. Megan makes
beaded necklaces; Andy rubs his hands obsessively
on his pants. (What kind of expression is that?
Shouldn't she give him a stress ball or something?
That's what Ms. Harrison would do.) Iggie, nothing
new, is making origami animals, and Daniel is drawing

huge penises and deformed vaginas in a sketch pad. It's very disturbing but I can't stop looking. He keeps looking over at me and smiling so I know he knows that I know what he's doing.

A moment ago, I stopped writing when I heard Lisa say that we were going to go around the room and share any dreams we've had lately. She's going to "interpret" these dreams to see if anything hidden in our subconscious is revealing something important to us. Oh, I can't wait for my turn. I am, right now, counting the tiles on the floor.

So Daniel's dream was hilarious, and I don't for a second think it is one he really had. Lisa is so dim because she gave it all kinds of attention. Daniel said he was wandering in the desert for forty days and forty nights (he's not a Jew), and all he came across were giant, tall, prickly cacti that he couldn't touch. He was starving and he knew the cacti had "juicy meat with gooey centers," but he couldn't touch them because of the stickers. In between the cacti in the sand were these oblong holes he kept jumping over because dangerous, biting snakes that squirted red venom were hidden inside. When he woke up, he realized he had a wet dream. (OMG.) Lisa turned all shades of embarrassed. She didn't ask him one question about penises and vaginas, which is totally what I would have done! Shit, it's my turn soon. I have to stop writing so I can fabricate a dream here.

CLASS ASSIGNMENT 3/27
Essay #13: Reflecting on the School Trip

(What I bravely turn in despite the fact that I know this is not the essay that Ms. Harrison is looking for. My winning grade streak is over. D.)

Danielle Levine

English 12

Ms. Harrison

Period 4

The administration of the school needs to get some perspective.

While it was way bad that James got that tattoo in Canterbury, it was not bad that you've had a tattoo on your wrist for I don't know how long. I can be sure that you did not get it while being chaperoned to another country. Your tattoo looks like a lovely flower bracelet, and it says something in another language that I don't know but that I am sure has real meaning for you.

Since the spring break, we've all noticed that you've been covering up your tattoo with a bandage. What we all used to just ignore has become a hot topic of conversation. I will admit that my mind drifted during your class as a result of that bandage. (I listened to what you said about *King Lear* as best I could, I want you to know, but the bandage was a major distraction.) Why is it covered now? What happened? We overheard some other teachers saying you got in trouble because James got a tattoo and the administration thinks it's your fault.

I can tell you right now that you weren't the reason James got the tattoo. James doesn't think that deep. He's just a free spirit.

Is the administration using you as a scapegoat? I don't want you to end up like Lee Harvey Oswald!

Teacher comments: *I wanted you to focus on your experience on the trip. No need to obsess on mine.*

#1 GOOD SCHOOL JOURNAL 3/28

(A real conversation with a classmate during the nutrition break)

While sitting alone at nutrition and putting the finishing touches on my NYC skyline that has turned in to a sweeping landscape across the table now that it's this late in the year, Keira sat down next to me with her books.

"Hey, Danielle, whoa, you'll have to sign that thing when you're done with it. I hope you don't mind if I sit here. I need to study and I need the vibe from someone smart in English so I can pass Harrison's vocabulary test today."

"No problem."

"Yeah, yikes, Harrison and the tattoo drama. Wait, let me use a vocab word here. It's *scandalous*."

"Good word. I know," I said. "We should do something, like, I don't know, all wear wrist bandages in *solidarity* or something to make a point."

"That is completely brilliant. I'm going to text everybody right now. We have to start doing that tomorrow. No question."

"Great." And I sat there as the most connected woman on campus contacted everyone and told 'em what's up before she went back to studying her vocab. I am sure they all texted her back, "As you wish."

JUSTINE LETTER 3/30
Letter from Justine to me

Dear Danielle,

How absolutely delightful to receive a letter from you! I just adore feeling a kinship with another part of the globe. It all feels so exciting. A girl like you who gets to take school trips to England from America must live a blessed life. You must take a moment right now to be grateful for such a thing.

Also, if you do find yourself lost in a melancholy field of thought from time to time, which I suspect may happen to the likes of you, please remember that it all moves. The sun comes up; the sun goes down. There is a rise and fall to all things. That is the journey of our lives. Journeys excite me so, which is why I love meeting wide-eyed travelers like you, those who embrace the experience with wonder.

Since you've left, I have given five more tours of Canterbury, but I have not met anyone as intriguing and special as you. No other pen pals are manifest. And, indeed, no one from any of the other groups got a tattoo down at Percy's shop the way the young man from your group did. What an adventurer, that one.

Please write and tell me how your days are being filled.

With a smile on my face,
Justine

CLASS ASSIGNMENT 4/3
Essay Assignment #14: The Car Wash Fund-raiser

(The version I write for myself right after the events unfold, not the version I turn in, which is boring but I earn an A because I write everything a teacher would want to hear about <u>altruism</u>, group work, and school spirit. It's so boring and fake, it can't even go in my collection. Completing that assignment was a total act of will after this terrible, terrible, terrible experience.)

Danielle Levine

English 12

Ms. Harrison

Period 4

On Saturday, the entire senior class had to come to school to participate in a school fund-raiser for the prom. We had to wash cars all day. I tried everything I could think of to get out of this event. In front of my mom, I obsessively counted my snow globes out loud and then started arranging the sea of crap in my room into strange piles so she might think I was coming unhinged and had to stay home. All she said was, "Oh, now you want to clean up this place? Well, use that energy to wash some cars." I told my father I thought today was a good day to stay in and read some medical journals together.

He said, "I love you, Danielle. Get out of the house."

A part of me really knew that today was going to be a disaster. "My fate cries out!" I put on the combat Chucks and a black conductor hat.

When my parents showed up to have their car washed, the boys there made comments about how hot Mom is. She is pretty, but it grosses me out and *diminishes* me totally that they notice.

Jacob arrived with Keira, Sara, Heather, John, and James around ten o'clock. He was dressed in a soft, solid-color, red T-shirt that makes him pop like a cutout figure in a fantasy book whose image is larger than the page can contain. Ms. Harrison left us for a while to go get doughnuts and drinks as we were doing fine on our own as she saw it.

As soon as Jacob got there and I saw him, I knew something was not right. His face was red, he was laughing, and he couldn't control his movements like he usually does. A boy of such smooth presence in the world had become a teetering doll. It couldn't have been clearer. He was drunk.

As I was taking him in, he pulled a flask out of his plaid shorts. "VODKA!" he screamed. A bunch of people took turns on the flask.

Jacob prowled around like the animal he was at this point. In some primal state, he started communicating with everyone as if they were the animals their essences exuded. He purred at Keira, who I was surprised to see drank from the flask, too. He lifted her onto a car while he kissed her, and a team of seniors sprayed them with the hose. They rolled in soapsuds. It was a triumphant, filmic moment—where the winners win, and are beautiful, and to keep the scales balanced and the cinema interesting, the losers must lose.

Everything from here followed in slow motion. Jacob grabbed his crotch in a display of manly pain and hissed wildly at James, who is, indeed, a snake. He grunted at Sara like an ape and then started moaning like he was a sick, dying animal; he pranced like a peacock amid a laughing gaggle of geesey-girl cheerleaders. For a second, I saw Keira look annoyed with Jacob, but I could tell, even she couldn't stop the force that was Jacob at this point. All his charisma was focused on putting on this show, and it was not going to be stopped.

He barked cruelly at Heather, as if she were a dog, but she bit back, and he slumped away whimpering. Right then, I thought to retreat, too, but I stayed. Who knows why. But I guess I wanted what was coming for me. He darted in my direction and stopped in front of me. Everything stopped. I had this feeling one other time in my life. Both times it was like I knew something very terrible was going to happen to me, and the wheels of the universe slowed down just a bit, so the impact of what was about to occur could be survived, if even just barely.

Jacob smiled slowly . . . and then, very deliberately, with crazed energy . . . he *moo'd*. "Mooooooo. Mooooooooo! Mooooooooooooooooo!!!!"

I have no idea how anyone reacted, but I imagine they all

laughed. Everything, the whole world hadn't come up to speed yet. I had loved Jacob for who knows how long, but a big fraction of my life, and here he was giving me the most honest communication he had ever given to me, and it was . . . disgust. The alcohol had erased all social constraints, and the God's honest truth was screaming around the parking lot.

It didn't matter that he thought I had cool eyes. It didn't matter that he had said he would rather touch me than drink toilet water. None of what I thought mattered did. I was wearing a bell around my neck. I was being led up the winding path to the slaughterhouse, unaware of the truth that always was before me. I was a fool to have ever thought, even for a second, otherwise. Deep down, in a true, ugly place inside of him, he thought that I was a cow. I thought I was, too, but I saw then, that so did the world, even someone I loved who I kept making excuses for. The truth, with all its edges, cut its way out.

He moved away from me and jumped like a jackrabbit over to one of his friends, who is a known whore. He just kept moving and my head started swimming. No one changed anything. They didn't stop washing, they didn't stop spraying or laughing or talking or seeing. At least it seemed that way to me.

I was lost in an internal episode of my own creation. Inside me, my heart was breaking in a way I hadn't known was possible, which was ironic because I thought when I was thirteen it had shattered completely, on that fucking bullshit horrible night when I offered no protection. But no, my heart just cracked like an earthquake then, fragile and splintered and precariously wobbly like a Jenga game. Now it was obliterated. One last move and all the pieces came crashing on the carpet. Game over.

And I feel guilty as hell, I hate me, for caring so much about my own fucking shatteredness when there are others who have had to endure so much worse still. Who am I?

Shards of my heart were scattered throughout the universe. My Tin Man self walked slowly backward into the girls' restroom without anyone knowing I was even gone, without anyone realizing that I was tapping into a world inside myself that I didn't know was there. It was dark and shadowy and scary as shit. The barnyard revelry continued outside in a world I had honored too much, that I had given the wrong kind of attention to. The dark abyss of my inside world was exploding so I would pay attention to it. I held on to the bathroom sink to steady myself while I shook uncontrollably. After the wave of terror passed, I reached into my pocket and felt my phone.

One of the first rituals Lisa had us do in social skills class was exchange phone numbers. That is what successfully social people do. I found Daniel in his proper alphabetical place in my phone directory, and I called him without even knowing why. We had this conversation:

"Hey, Daniel. It's Danielle from your social skills class. Isn't it kinda weird that our names are the male and female versions of each other?"

"Yeah. Lisa would be proud of you for starting the conversation in such a provocative way. What are you doing?"

"Oh, nothing. You want to meet me at the Galleria for lunch?"

"Sure. An hour?"

"Perfect."

I'm sort of stunned at my utter calmness on the outside while an implosion was happening on the inside. It's amazing that a human being can be this obviously dual. I decided to walk the short distance from school to the Galleria. I managed to write all this down before I left. Just getting it all down is a relief. Some things are so awful they don't fit anywhere inside you. They deserve to just be symbols on a page instead.

ME-MOIR JOURNAL 4/4
After the car wash
After I had a day to hash it all out

I met Daniel at the Galleria right on schedule. We walked around and grabbed some lunch to go and sat down by the big outdoor fountain and ate. He said the only thing going on at his house was a pool party his stepdad was throwing for church friends. When his mom remarried, the whole family had to become Catholic. He had to do a lot of perfunctory standing, kneeling, praying, admitting, denying, and withholding. He told me he thought it was one of the funniest religions around and he'd go along for the comedy factor. Every Sunday he has to wait in line for someone to place a flat piece of bread on his tongue. He makes sure his tongue is filled with saliva, and his fly is open when he goes through this ritual. Sometimes he lets out the faintest, audible little grunt. Then, once a week he begs his stepdad to take him to confession.

Sal, his stepdad, thinks Daniel is really benefiting from the conversion and loves taking him to confession. Daniel, on the other hand, uses the confessional to have "secret boners" as he says. He wants me to go with him and sit in the dark box and see what it does to me because it gets him hard every time for reasons that defy explanation. He keeps a list of made-up sins he can tell the priest so he's always got conversation when he's in there. The more elaborate or creative the sin, the better.

One time he told the priest he had stolen money from the school cafeteria after weeks of planning and mapping out his heist—very premeditated—and buried it behind the scoreboard on the field. He went on to say he forgot to dig it up and had been home with the flu and was worried some asshole would get to it before he did. (He had to say a litany of prayers for the theft and the recent swearing.) When Daniel went to school the next day, the maintenance crew was digging behind the scoreboard! So much for sinner/priest confidentiality.

I said that the priest may not keep secrets but at least he didn't molest you! Daniel said he was hoping to get molested because then he could sue the church and go to college and live off the money for a while using some of it for therapy to deal with the shame. I said that was a super-sized serving of wrong, and Daniel said he knew that, but college was expensive and so desperate measures needed considering.

After confession and the prayers he has to say, he tells Sal he needs to go be alone in his room to contemplate all he's done that week that was sinful. Then he goes to his room, locks the door, knows he won't be disturbed, and "takes himself on a date." He says confession builds up all this awesome tension he needs to release.

Sal really loves him, he says, and he likes the guy, too, but their relationship is based on a bunch of lies like so much is. If they told the truth to each other it would destroy this fiction that is working so well.

During dessert, I told Daniel about what happened with Jacob at the car wash. He said Jacob was an asshole, which I already knew at that point, but no amount of icing on any cake could completely cover the twisted, complicated feelings I had. I would hate him, truly, for the rest of my life for the *moo*-ing, but another part of me still held on, not my heart—which had been obliterated because this person I had *deified*, honored, lusted after, all that crap, was not worth loving. Where would I go with all those emotions that I spent on him?

Daniel suggested that I spend them on me.

Huh?

"Look, your life has been hard enough up to this point. You are worth a million million Jacob Kingstons. You're the ton of kings, not him. You just got a little confused and saw in him what you should have seen in yourself. Anyone would be

143

clouded by reality when they've lived through what you did."

"What are you talking about, Daniel?"

"You know."

"No. I don't."

"Danielle, we went to the same school then, before we both moved. I know the deal. You know I do."

"What school?"

"Cut the shit, Danielle. I was in your eighth-grade class at Jefferson Middle School down in Orange County. I lived there before my mom and dad split up. You remember, right? I knew you and Emily. I was really upset about the whole thing. I sent you that collage with the poem. Jesus, I thought that's why you were so friendly to me in the social skills class, why you stared at me the first class. I thought you remembered me from before you moved and changed schools."

From an even deeper place than where my heart had been, an energy of flight rose up. Before I even knew what I was doing, I got up and ran. I ran onto the sidewalk of Ventura Boulevard and kept running. I ran across every street corner without stopping for any traffic signals. I wished so much I could fly. I heard a car screech and a man scream at me. I knocked over a skateboarder who was in my way. I tripped on a magazine that littered the sidewalk, and I just got up and kept going even though my knee was cut and blood was dripping down my leg. The pain felt good. I screamed along with a song that was pounding out of a car stereo. I sobbed and sobbed and sobbed, swallowing air by the gallons and thrusting it out in loud chokes. I cried until my eyes burned and I couldn't see a damn thing in front of me. I didn't care. Nothing was worth seeing. It was all useless. "Tis an unweeded garden that grows to seed. Things rank in nature possess it merely." I ran nonstop for four miles and all the way up my hill until I fell onto the front lawn of my house. I started ripping out the perfect grass and the roses my mother prized so highly. I rubbed dirt all over my face. My hands bled along with my knee. I threw myself on my back and looked up at the sky and screamed louder than I thought possible.

I didn't realize that Daniel had run the entire way behind me until I felt my mother, my father, and Daniel hold me in the grass. My father scooped me up and carried me to my room while he softly sang in my ear and rubbed my hair out of my face. I let all of me float along with his song until the melody took me to sleep.

ME-MOIR JOURNAL 4/5
About what happened after eating dirt

My mother made me breakfast this morning, the day after I came running home. She smiled at me as she cooked and it drove me mad. I hate when she feels sorry for me.

"Honey, you know how I name all the hummingbirds that come to feed? Well, there are a group of three new birds with fuchsia-colored heads. They are truly magnificent. I'm considering calling them 'the fuchsia-head gang.' What do you, think?" I knew she was trying to brighten the mood, but I ignored her.

"Well, is this what you expected when you adopted a daughter? Is this what you thought you'd get?"

"Danielle, in so many ways, you are so much better than I could have ever imagined."

"Yeah, right."

"We all have times in our lives where it is hard to keep it together."

"Thank God Dad played rugby in college. Otherwise, he'd never have been able to carry me to bed."

My mom smiled at me again.

"Your friend Daniel told us what happened at the car wash. I'm truly sorry. Jacob Kingston is a little shit, isn't he?" I had never heard my beautiful mother swear like that. It was fantastic. I looked up from my lap.

"Yes, Mother, he damn right is."

"Okay, lady. Let's not push it."

So we actually laughed a little, and then we went to yoga together. Toward the end of class, when we were all hot and in a zone, David gave one of his inspirational talks and today it really sank in there, in the empty place in me that I was going to have to refill with things more meaningful than before. He said things need to get really hot before they can be transformed. Anything in your life that can burn is worth burning.

Wow, there is so much inside me that is on fire and some

things I strangely don't want to burn. I don't want to let my feelings for Jacob burn away. He gave me something to long for, to fantasize about, and I wanted to think he loved my eyes. I wanted to hold on to the fact that his hands had been where no one else's had, even though I can't think that for long because it makes me sick after it makes me blush. It is all a dull ache that is now going to be a scorching flame for a little bit. Well, I don't really know for how long, but I'm hoping just a little bit. (I think I'm fooling myself for comfort and out of hope.)

But, and this is really true: I don't want everything I remember about Emily to burn away. What kind of true friend would I be if I let all that I know and love about her disintegrate? But the way David said it, and the way it settled in the empty cavity that was once my heart, I know I am going to have to come to a greater understanding of what he means. I am going to have to let things burn.

My mother has never done this before, but she's letting me take a week off school. She said that in exchange, I had to talk to Marv on the phone. So I did.

"Danielle, are you hanging in there?" Marv asked.

"I guess so."

"I am sure it's tough."

"Yeah. I know you had a woman laugh in your face and throw furniture at you, but you never had the boy of your dreams *moo* in your face."

"Indeed, Danielle. Indeed. Tell me how that whole experience made you feel."

"Lost."

"Hmmm. That is understandable and well said. You may not believe me, but you are in a very powerful place. It's not until we are lost that we can be found."

And now I am just sitting here for a minute trying to let his words settle within me and hoping a big burp of understanding rises about that and the burning.

AUNT JOYCE E-MAIL 4/6
E-mail from Aunt Joyce after she learns her niece is a cow

Well, Danielle, I'm just gonna be honest. I want to kill that kid you like. I know these aren't adult feelings, but I don't care for the moment. My very wise, adorable therapist once told me that Carl Jung said, "You can be a fool and fall in love or you can miss out on all life has to offer." So you were a fool. Good for you. Bravo. Join the painful club I've been a part of for twenty-some years. How proud of you I am to have you as a member; I cannot find words.

For a little while be beloved. The loving can wait. Let your father, your mother, and me love you. Know you are beloved. And, oh, how you are. I love every little hair on your gorgeous self. You're perfect.

Because I love you and know what you can withstand, I will
not call Jacob's parents and tell them that we are coming
over so he can apologize to you. That is what I want to
do, however. You deserve an apology from him. Actually,
Danielle, you deserve much, much more than you have
decided you do.

Jacob doesn't serve you. Don't take the cup from him any
longer. Put it down. There is another you can drink from.
Inside you is a two-million-year-old soul that knows what you
deserve, that's making martinis as we speak. Start talking to
that woman and drink what she's serving.

Your Forever Aunt Joyce.

AUNT JOYCE E-MAIL 4/6
E-mail from me to Aunt Joyce

Dearest Forever Aunt Joyce,

Thanks for being so smart. What would I do if I didn't have
you to love me? I don't know. I know everything you said
is true, but it will take me a while to *really* know. My heart
is broken. It's broken. Well, it's more than that—it's gone.
This plan that God has worked out for life just doesn't seem
doable. I'm kinda pissed off about it. Teeth, for one thing.

Why would a deity design teeth to rot? I got a cavity that needs to be filled on top of everything else. It seems like added insult to injury. Well, I gotta go because a guy from my social skills class is coming over, and we're gonna do homework together. His name is Daniel. I'm probably not telling you anything you don't know because you and Mom seem to always have all the up-to-date info on my life. Thanks, though, you save me.

Danielle (aka Clarabelle, the cow)

ME-MOIR JOURNAL 4/8
The morning after Daniel came over

I'm really miserable. I mean, I have to be. Jacob Kingston *moo*'d in my face. It's ridiculous to write, but it's completely painful to feel. If I could lobotomize this experience from my brain, do an eternal-sunshine-of-the-spotless-mind overhaul on the whole episode, and every warm feeling I ever had for Jacob, I would in a hot second.

Daniel came over and brought his homework, and we both sat at the kitchen table and did work. He tried to apologize for the Emily thing, but I told him to stop. He had nothing to apologize for. I had a bunch of my hats scattered on the table, and I think he was trying to cheer me up, but he put on a fashion show with them. It made us both laugh to see him in the feathered bonnet I have, the one with flowers around the rim.

"I remember how funny you and Emily were together in junior high," he said.

I was uncomfortable for a minute but then I said, "You do? We were?"

"Yeah. I remember this one day in seventh grade when we all got balloons for some reason. You know, the helium kind on strings. And you and Emily drew faces with mustaches on yours and pretended they were your rich husbands. You carried those escorts around all day. It was classic juvenile hilarity."

"I forgot about that."

"I admired you both. Smart ladies in the market for rich men . . . those are girls to watch, I thought." He punctuated the statement perfectly by flipping the Sherlock Holmes–style hat onto his head.

Talking about Emily and talking with Daniel made me realize just how long it has been since I have had a friend. And maybe that's what Daniel is becoming for me, a friend. I mean, he ran four miles in pursuit of my crazy self and hugged me after I ate dirt. That's gotta be a friend, right?

After we finished our work, my mom made us dinner. I could tell my mom liked Daniel, and it was a little embarrassing how proper she was and how she got out my favorite plates, the ones that have European landmarks and postage designs; they look like old postcards, and I fell in love with them on a family trip years ago, so Mom bought them for me. She served us salmon and asparagus. As a side note, I'd like to add that we haven't had any red meat since the incident.

When dinner was over, Mom excused herself to go to her own therapy appointment while Dad worked out at the office gym. (God, what is it with my family? Every single one of us has a therapist and a *myriad* of self-help regimens! I have no idea what my dad even talks about in his therapy because he seems so together all the time, but he goes.)

I was alone in the house with Daniel. I had never been alone in my house with a boy EVER. We went into the living room because Daniel brought *Harold and Maude* for us to watch together. Daniel had no idea how much I love this movie, but he loves it, too. We sang along to the sound track, and I cried a little at the end, but so did Daniel. "Don't look at me," he half joked. "Leave me alone with my rich emotions." And then I punched him in the arm and that led to him dragging me onto the floor where we wrestled and tickled each other until we were exhausted.

When my mom came home, she made Daniel call his mom and say he was spending the night. It was a school night, and I don't know how our parents let this happen, but he stayed, and he slept on my couch and so did I. I fell asleep for the first time in a boy's arms. As I started to close my eyes, I stared out at the entire San Fernando Valley through our big living room window. The dark, starry sky was the perfect blanket for us; the mysterious universe snuggling us in. I don't know why my mom didn't wake me up and make me get into bed. I don't know. But my dreams in those hours were so soft and lyrical. I dreamed I was lying on a giant soft pillow that swallowed me and gave off oxygen. The farther I buried my face in it, the more life I felt.

When my mom woke us up at six, she gave Daniel towels and walked him toward the shower. He dressed in the clothes he came over in, but he looked cool. We ate fruit and toast and talked about how we had to face Lisa and the rest of the misfits tonight in social skills class. We decided we'd pretend we both went to the rock concert that his stepfather was at last night, and therefore, couldn't hear anything from tinnitus and couldn't speak due to our screaming-induced laryngitis; but Lisa would have to be thrilled as we had "made a social date." My mom packed him a lunch (which I just loved), I hugged him good-bye, and my mother drove him to school while I stayed home and started this journal. I have never loved my mom so much. However, I don't want to mischaracterize anything. I'm still profoundly miserable.

ME-MOIR JOURNAL 4/12
Another Journal about Daniel

Daniel came over one more time before I went back to school. He actually volunteered to go to Meadow Oaks and pick up all my homework from the front office so I wouldn't get too behind; there isn't that much school left and I can't jeopardize my college options. Daniel found me in my room reading, and he looked around at all my stuff.

"Holy crap, Danielle. I can't believe you've read all these books."

"How do you know I actually read them?"

"It's obvious. All the pages are dog-eared and the covers are all worn. Oh my God, you're a genius."

"Oh, but I wish," I said.

I showed him my letter from Justine. He thought it was awesome. "She is wicked wise," he said and "you are lucky to be friends with someone who has been alive a long, long time. But you know what I like best about her? The fact that she likes you. 'Cause that club, the digging Danielle club—we're the shit."

I threw my arms around him.

"It's true. I have good taste," he said.

He insisted we call each other when I got back in school to make sure I'm feeling "copacetic" when I'm in class with Jacob. I'm glad he set that up because back at school, after fourth period, I ran out into the quad and called him.

"I was just in English with him. It was really hard. Looking at him makes me sick to my stomach."

Daniel said, "Abide, sister, abide."

"Abide what? Him?"

"Yes! Abide it all. Him. The situation. Endure it. Withstand it."

"I'll try, but I'm afraid I might puke."

"Well, if you think you are going to, try to make it to Jacob's lap."

"Ha! Good plan. Thank you."

Talking to Daniel on the phone made it look like I had a friend. I saw Sara do a double take when she saw me on the phone laughing, and I realized it didn't just *look like* I had a friend. I actually did.

ME-MOIR JOURNAL 4/13

Jesus, can't social skills class just go away??!!!

No, it cannot, according to my mother who says these classes have "yielded some fine results. Look at your friendship with Daniel," and so I have to keep going because it might get even better. I told her I don't need it to get any better. This is good. I have a friend. Social skills class—a success. "Not so fast," she says.

When I'm forced to do stuff against my will like this I want to be destructive and ruin environments. I want to fully turn on my impulsivity spigot so that all the inappropriate words I have stuffed in my head flow out. If I actually loosen this spigot in social skills class in an effort to show my mother how bad this class is for me and punish her at the same time, I realize I will probably just end up in some other group I can't stand or have to go for an evaluation to see if I have Tourette's syndrome. (If I had to have a syndrome, I think I would like to have that one, but Daniel said I'm being very shortsighted with that view, that Tourette's is nothing to shout about. He's funny.) So I went to class tonight, and I swear, if it weren't for Daniel, I might gouge my eyes out with one of Lisa's brooches (like Oedipus, thank you very much) right in front of everyone, and they could just send me to wander into the desert of Los Angeles!

Tonight we had to do what Lisa calls a "social autopsy." We had to each talk about a social situation in our lives that we didn't think went well, and Lisa took it apart and analyzed it like doctors do to dead bodies. I think the analogy is morbid and hopeless. A social autopsy? Really? Like we're all dead on arrival in any social situation. That is probably true, but how messed up for Lisa to use this language. Some of us in the room get the deep, dark, penetrating meaning.

Daniel saw the schedule for tonight online where Lisa posts everything for us. I just ignore it, but Daniel gets off on checking it out and mocking it. He's more evolved than me, clearly. Anyway, he saw that we were doing social autopsies tonight and he came in dressed as a cadaver. A stroke of genius, totally. He put gray makeup all over his face that made him look plastic, and, well, dead, and said he came prepared for his autopsy. It was fantastic. We all laughed, and I have to give it to Lisa because instead of acting all offended and superior like she usually would, she laughed, too.

For his autopsy Daniel told a story about being slammed

156

up against his locker by a football player at school, and how the incident drew a crowd. He couldn't fight back, and there were a bunch of people who just saw him slide down his locker onto the floor and wipe snot and blood off his nose. He just started singing "Who Let the Dogs Out?", which I thought was a brilliant maneuver in this situation, but it got him further pummeled.

"Analyze that situation, Doctor," he said to Lisa.

At first, I didn't know if this really happened to Daniel or if he was just using it to make Lisa struggle at her craft. Lisa asked if Daniel had done anything that might have instigated that assault (not that anything would justify that behavior she said); she was just asking. Daniel said he didn't have the slightest idea what he had done.

I could tell by the way Daniel said it that he knew exactly what caused the football player to go crazy, but he wasn't going to tell Lisa. I had a feeling then that this was a true story. I don't remember what Lisa said to Daniel. I don't think I was listening at that point because my mind started drifting off and thinking about how Daniel has had it rough, too. I wasn't the only person in the room whose life had been marked by pain and for whom school was a war zone.

Essay assigned by me to me to vent my frustration 4/18
Why Must Things Like This Always Happen

Danielle Levine

English 12

Ms. Harrison

Period 4

In English class today, I was staring out the corner window and found myself taken in by a little hummingbird fluttering among the huge branches of the tree that grows outside our second-floor classroom. It was gray and for a second I wondered if this was the hummingbird my mom called Spaulding. It made me chuckle, and I wasn't paying attention when Ms. Harrison announced our groups for the day. Keira yelled my name to break my trance, and that's when I found out my group consisted of me, Keira, and Jacob. Need I write more? Do those three names not clearly address the title of this essay I assigned myself? Even though I like Keira, it's really hard for me to be around her and Jacob, especially since they found every excuse to touch each other in between discussing the assignment, which was to brainstorm-as-a-group possible ideas for a "poignant and passionate" essay entitled "Why I Stand Out." I thought "murder-suicide in front of your classmates" would fit the bill, but I kept that idea to myself.

I was completely infuriated that Jacob just talked to me as

if everything was as it always was—which it frickin' was for him because his *moo*-ing in my face had no impact on him at all!!!!!!!!!!! (There aren't enough exclamation points in the world, believe me.) And I realize that I am tragically flawed because I can't just get over this easily; that I can't let it all roll off my back; that I can't figure out how to be like the Amish who can forgive so easily. Dear God, right now, can't you teach me how to do that? What kind of God designed a world where things and people you find value in eventually hurt you?

I really wish someone could give me a clear, *cogent* response to that question.

During the course of our little perverse brainstorming session, Jacob said to me, "Danielle, why don't you write about how you have red hair? That makes you stand out."

Yes, and why don't I also add to this winner of an essay how I'm fat! Ah, Jacob, Ye of the genius literary mind.

He told Keira, "Hey, babe, you should write about your tongue. That stands out." She hit him, thank goodness. That let out a little steam from my desire to bludgeon him.

I logically see what a jerk Jacob can be, but that doesn't seem to be enough to get my body from having charged feelings for him. OMG, I could solve the energy crisis with the feelings this guy stirs up in me!

To make matters worse, at one point, Keira said, "Danielle, do you have a date to prom? Because Jacob has a friend who wants to go, and he's like just a little chubby but super nice. Do you want to go with him?"

159

"No, but thanks. I'm going with my boyfriend."

What the hell was I thinking? I don't know, but now I have to remember to ask Daniel to be my pretend boyfriend for prom.

I hate my crazy emotions, and I hate the God that made this emotional chaos possible. Oh, and I *tangentially* hate the teacher who put me face-to-face with the object of all my conflict. During class, I heard my father's voice say, "Danielle, work is the antidote for worry." This was a little past worry, Dad, and trying to work in that situation was impossible. I didn't come up with any good ideas for that ridiculous essay.

ME-MOIR JOURNAL 4/23

Daniel and I watch The Big Lebowski

Daniel and I stayed up too late on Friday night and watched a movie he insisted I see. It was called *The Big Lebowski*, and he said if I watched it I would learn to abide in the proper way, and I would laugh heartily, which I did. The movie was *revelatory*.

First off, I saw that people have problems that never even occurred to me. Cutting off your toe to make money is beyond nuts. Also, I had no idea that people take bowling so seriously. It was really an obsession with these people. Beyond all the craziness, there was something so enticing about this film. It may be that it had mythic elements, which is something we are talking about in English right now.

Myths are these universal stories that come about and last and last over thousands of years because everyone can relate to them. We have mythic symbols and mythic relationships that just are. It's kinda amazing to me. A hero is a mythic symbol. In a way, Jeff Bridges is a hero in that movie—albeit, a very lazy one. The narrator with the really cool deep voice says "He's the man for his time and place" and in Los Angeles, nonetheless.

Anyway, Daniel and I talked like Maude Lebowski for hours after that movie. I have the affected accent pretty much down. "The story's ludicrous" is now one of my favorite things to say because, not only does it apply to the plot lines of porno films, which is what Maude was referring to when she said it, but "The story's ludicrous" might as well be the bumper sticker on the vehicle that is my life given that I was *moo*'d at publicly. Daniel had gone to Lebowski Fest a few years ago and said we had to go this year because there was one near us. Okay, Dude, I'm in!

It's held at a bowling alley and you dress up as characters from the movie, and Daniel said everyone is incredibly creative in their choices. We'd have to rewatch the movie and look for über-subtle details in order to come up with a costume because that is what some people do, and it's fun to try to guess what people are. (He said the more obvious ones are fun, too, but we are clearly the nuanced, obscure types.) If truth be told, I'm looking for any events or distractions to keep my mind off graduating from high school and going on to more school where I'll continue to feel like a freak. (At least at Lebowski Fest everyone is a freak.)

Daniel and I have been talking about college a lot. I got in to three of the six schools that I applied to. I think my mom is more excited than I am about my college options because she's been reading about them online constantly and creating lengthy, color-coded pros and cons lists. Every time I talk to her about it, I just end up confused over her color-coding, which she tells me is not "the salient point" from her notes.

Daniel applied to the California universities like I did because his parents made him, and he didn't have to write an essay or send a teacher recommendation, which he said wouldn't help his chances. He was thinking of applying to some private Catholic schools because of his weird fetish for Catholicism, and while Sal appreciated his devotion (little did he know), he said they were too expensive. At any rate, we have to decide on schools soon because we have to send in our deposits. However, figuring out how to go to Lebowski Fest sounds more fun at the moment.

AUNT JOYCE E-MAIL 4/24

Dear Super-Hip, Way Cool Aunt Joyce,

I really need you to watch *The Big Lebowski*, think it is one of the best movies ever, and then want to take Daniel and me to Lebowski Fest. I'll explain the thing to you after you watch the movie and make my dream come true! (I'm sure we need someone over twenty-one to take us. You just barely fit that bill, LOL.)

Your niece who loves you soooooooooooo much,
Danielle

AUNT JOYCE E-MAIL 4/24
E-mail back from Aunt Joyce just seconds later

Well, lady, I'll watch the movie, research Lebowski Fest, and then let you know.

A.J.

JUSTINE LETTER
Letter to Justine

Dear Justine,
   Thank you for writing me. I hope you don't mind that I shared your letter with my friend Daniel, who I think is my best friend, and you are the first person I'm telling.
   How am I filling my days, you asked? Well, right now I'm trying to get over a boy I once really liked but who acted like a real jerk to me on several occasions,

actually. And I'm also being forced to think about college and where I will go. My friend Daniel and I are going to talk about it and try to come up with a plan. I never spent much time thinking beyond high school because dealing with high school was hard enough, and there were some bad things that happened before high school that made thinking about the future kind of an incidental idea. I don't know if that makes sense. My life is kind of complicated, I guess. So, anyway, I guess I'm busy with thoughts.

I am also sometimes busy with hanging out with Daniel or with going to yoga with my mom or doing other family things. (I have a really cool aunt, and if I could grow up and be remotely like her, I'd be thrilled. I would also be thrilled to be like you, too.)

I like my yoga class. I'm trying to lose a little weight. The teacher says some really smart things, which reminds me that I saw some quotes you had written and put on your refrigerator. One said, "Close both eyes to see with the other. ~Rumi." Did your husband write that? Is "Rumi" Bubbles's real name? He was smart. Anyway, I hope you are doing great. I sure like knowing you.

Love,
Danielle

CLASS ASSIGNMENT 4/27
Essay that answers this prompt: Pick a work
of literature we've read this year and a movie
you've seen and discuss their mythic/symbolic
messages.

(I loved this assignment! Ms. Harrison made up for
pairing me with Keira and Jacob; all is not lost! I
spent a lot of time writing this essay—with Daniel,
admittedly—but I thought what we wrote rocked.
Ms. Harrison only thought it rocked a B because I
used the word <u>screwed</u>, was too informal in places,
used personal pronouns, had too many parentheticals,
didn't cite my quotes properly, and "summarized"
where I should have "analyzed" the movie. Really and
truly, sometimes teachers have no give. They are so
damned rigid in what they want in their essays. If she
just read this thing as a person and not as a teacher,
she might have gotten it and not let her "thinking get
too uptight" LOL.)

Danielle Levine
English 12
Ms. Harrison
Period 4

My favorite works of literature have mythic structures. The

hero (tragic or otherwise) appears, is confronted with a problem, gets lost, and eventually finds his way home or to some symbol of home. There are specific lessons in myths, revealed through symbols that can carry us through our lives. Their messages are universal.

King Lear is one of these stories. In *King Lear*, a hapless king divides his kingdom amid three daughters. *Two* shower him with the words of praise he seeks, while his third is unable to "heave her heart into her mouth." She is only able to love the king simply, as her bond requires, "no more, no less." Wooed by the flattering words of the eldest two, the king divides his kingdom between them and leaves the youngest nothing. (Poor Cordelia.) He is ultimately *undone* by this choice. He would have done better to see the truth in the simple, honest feelings of his youngest.

The three daughters symbolize the things we create in the world and that we find meaning through. Sometimes it is too easy to think we will find meaning and purpose in the choices that are flashy or flattering or shiny like gold. (Like really cute boys.) But those things lose their luster, so it is best not to invest in them. They do not possess a lasting value. In Lear's case, he actually gets royally screwed by them! (Pun totally intended.)

A kingdom is a metaphor for one's soul, the Self. We end up disappointed if we divide up our kingdom to false daughters. Sometimes, what is real, true, and meaningful is smaller, gentler, and quieter than we think. (Sometimes it is a new friend who is better than the other kind of love you thought you wanted.) It is no easy task to figure out when and how to divide your kingdom wisely, how to give of yourself (let the spigots loose) or how to not give of yourself. (Sometimes yourself just seems to leak out all over the place.) This is the *daunting* task of every person, and I am trying to find all the grace and the foresight to choose well, so I find myself with a thriving *queendom* (my own new vocabulary word). I have not always chosen well by any means.

Another example of a mythic story is from the world of movies: *The Big Lebowski*. If you haven't seen it, do so. If you have, watch it again. It gets better with repeat viewings (just like Shakespeare).

The Big Lebowski is a very good comedic film, but it is also another mythic story whose lessons are important. In it, our laid-back, unlikely hero, The Dude, is thrust into a situation of mistaken identity and chaos ensues. Occasionally throughout the story, The Dude becomes lost and unhinged—he becomes impatient and worried, not usual traits of his. To quote a supporting character, he starts "being very *un*dude." It happens to the best of us, I'm learning. (King Lear becomes very undude during and after he *abdicates* power.) Eventually realizing that his own "thinking has become very uptight," The Dude soon eases back into his calm, clever self, and situations begin to work themselves out for our hero. Ultimately, His Dudeness tells us that "The Dude abides." Gosh, but I really, really needed that bit of wisdom.

To abide means to wait for, to stand ready for, to stand up

under, to endure, to withstand. And because The Dude abides, for the most part, the truth comes to light and the chaos dissipates. King Lear did not abide and look what happened there. As The Dude says, "That's a bummer, man." No matter what life you choose, no matter where you divide your kingdom, you will have to abide many things. And you will hardly be able to avoid the ridiculous. Someone might even *moo* in your face one day. And you'll have to figure out how to handle that.

To abide is to take a stance of grace *and* power. It says to the universe that you recognize that all is not certain, that things constantly change, but that you are willing to participate and stay true to your own character *and* its evolution; and that you recognize you are smart enough and strong enough to do just that at the proper moment in time. Well, I think that is true of the idea of abiding, but it's a new concept to me, so you can let me know if I'm wrong.

All in all, we should go out and spread our kingdoms, our wealth of character, regardless of praise or compliment, or if we are *moo*'d at, and then do our best to abide what comes because heroes need to travel and have experiences in order to come home again as renewed men (or women).

ME-MOIR JOURNAL 4/28

(I noticed I have stopped numbering and for some reason am not nervous about that.)

Because Lisa says we should write down our dreams
Because maybe we'll figure something out from them

Last night I dreamed I was a *turbid* pool of water. I was aware that my boundaries were no longer human; that I didn't have the shape or movement of a human being, but I did have its consciousness. As this muddied pool of water, I was ashamed of my dirtiness. I knew that there were other bodies of water more magnificent and clear and clean. But I was what I was. I moved along a mossy bank and traveled effortlessly forward. At one point far along in my travels, I hit a massive mountain of rock. In my clouded state, I crashed against the jagged rocks and felt dizzy. Jostled, churning, and wild, my natural move-ment was deterred. For what felt like eternity, I slammed up against the rock. Slam. Slam. Slam. Slam. I couldn't fight the force of such a solid mass. I thought, well, here I come to stay. Here I must, like Sisyphus, repeat a scenario of endless torture. I couldn't or didn't cry or scream; I had all the properties of water. At one point, even though I thought I was thoroughly trapped, a part of me seeped into minute crevices in the rock bit by bit. This took forever. Droplet by droplet, hour by hour, I moved all of me into the mountainous rock and onto the other side. Slowly, my consciousness as water found itself in a crisp, clean glacial pool. It was huge. My muddiness was no match for the pristine waters in which I now found myself. I was no longer clouded. What I was had changed. I sensed myself amid this new atmosphere. I was cooler, smoother and more slow moving, but I was still moving. The bank I moved along was more solid, a calmer ride. Eventually, I hit an area thick with trees. We, I sensed myself as that, we, moved together under the earth where the trees were growing. I drenched the roots and slid along all the life below the surface. I would keep going, even though I didn't know where.

JUSTINE LETTER

Danielle,

Ah, Bubbles will forever be known as Bubbles to me. That quote, the one you read on my refrigerator, was by the poet Rumi, a true visionary from the thirteenth century. In this letter, I'd like to answer you with my favorite Rumi poem. He says all I would say to you, but he says it better. I hope you enjoy it.

The Guest House

This being human is a guest house.
Every morning a new arrival.

A joy, a depression, a meanness,
Some momentary awareness comes
As an unexpected visitor.
Welcome and entertain them all!
Even if they're a crowd of sorrows,
Who violently sweep your house
Empty of its furniture,
Still, treat each guest honorably.
He may be clearing you out
For some new delight.
The dark thought, the shame, the malice,
Meet them at the door laughing,
And invite them in.
Be grateful for whoever comes,
Because each has been sent
As a guide from beyond.

Rumi by way of Justine

ME-MOIR JOURNAL 5/4

*Immediately following Justine's letter, which I showed
to Daniel and he loved it, too*

Justine is proof that old people know things. I read that
poem twenty times already. I think it might be my new obsession. I taped it on my bathroom mirror and am going to read
it every day before school and hope that I can come to honor
the mean houseguest that is Jacob (and, unfortunately, others).
I wish I hadn't invited Jacob in, but I did. I guess Rumi would
have told me I gotta try to honor him now. Deep breath. I'm
gonna try. Rumi said those words a long time ago. That lets
me know there were douchebags then, too. It has to be or he
wouldn't have written that rockin' poem.

CLASS ASSIGNMENT 5/5
Expanded Quote Essay

(Ms. Harrison is not happy with me. I turn this essay
in and I really like it. I thought I followed all the rules
of the assignment—outside source, parenthetical
documentation etc.—but she was VERY frustrated
with me and my writing style, which she said is not
appropriate for these types of essays. I have to
stay in at lunch for a week and rewrite the thing
according to her sterile rules. I am not happy with how
the second draft is going so I won't be keeping it in
my collection.)

Danielle Levine

English 12

Ms. Harrison

Period 4

The quote from a piece of literature we read this year that I
decided to use as a jumping off point for this essay is "There
are more things in heaven and earth, Horatio, than are dreamt
of in your philosophy." (*Hamlet*, Act I, scene v, lines 187–188)
Such an idea has basically been reflected in my entire life, but
my father gave me some information the other night that really
hit that idea home for me in a richer way.

My father told me about this guy Paul Pearsall who wrote a

book in 1988 called *The Heart's Code*. (My dad has read some amazing things.) Anyway, in this book, this girl gets a heart transplant from another girl who had been murdered, and the girl who gets the heart wakes up and screams in the middle of the night after having nightmares where she recognizes the man who murdered the girl who gave her the heart. Shut up! That is incredible. Who would have ever thought something like that could happen? That is what Hamlet is talking to Horatio about.

Another guy in the book got a heart transplant and then started using the word *copacetic* all the time when he had never used it before. Turns out, the guy he got his heart from used that word all the time!!!! (I have to use a bunch of exclamation points here to make it clear just how amazing I think this is.) (Pearsall, 1988, pp. 7–8) Also, it is very ironic, the use of the word *copacetic,* because my friend Daniel taught me that word recently.

The implications of this kind of thing are incredible. First of all, things get stored in our bodies not just our minds. That made me rethink everything about what we know about consciousness. We understand so very little. We run around thinking we have things figured out, that we have control over things, and we don't even know that who we are lives everywhere in us. This was a real revelation to me because I've been heartbroken. (I don't want to go into the details of that with you, Ms. Harrison. Let the record just show that it's true.) I thought my heart had been obliterated, and I was sort of looking forward to going numb. But that didn't fully happen for me, and I think it's because all my heart wasn't just kept in my heart. It's in other places in me, too. I'd have to probably cut off all my limbs, poke out my eyes and maybe disembowel myself to get rid of the hurt. I am going to come up with another plan for dealing with my pain.

We don't understand how our bodies work, how we think, or why we are even here. If those questions are unanswerable, I realize there are so many more that are, too. But we pretend like things are figurable (I know that's not a word but please let me use it because it's perfect here). Remnants of feeling must be in all the cells.

We are much bigger and more complicated than I thought. That's what I really wanted to say in this essay. That's the crux of what Hamlet tells Horatio. It's something we should all embrace. I'm trying to, but I get stuck in smallness and worry and pain. I hope I can house other things in places in my body besides those negative ideas. I hope magic, peace, and laughter get stowed away in me, and if anyone ever gets a piece of me from a transplant, they can benefit, too. I hope that is my legacy even if I don't fully understand how it may come to be.

MARV MISSIVE
Letter from Marv to me

How are things, Danielle?

MARV MISSIVE
Letter from me to Marv

Do you think everyone has a Sisyphean rock they shove up a hill day after day?

MARV MISSIVE
Letter from Marv to me

Danielle, I think we all do at some point in our lives. I think we push that thing up every single day until we get tired of it and we stop.

MARV MISSIVE
Letter from me to Marv

Okay. Thanks, Marv.

MARV MISSIVE
Letter from Marv to me

You don't have to push the thing alone forever either.

MARV MISSIVE
Letter from me to Marv

I know. I'm not.

MARV MISSIVE
Letter from Marv to me

Okay. That's good to know.

AUNT JOYCE E-MAIL 5/8
E-mail to Aunt Joyce

Forever Aunt Joyce,

Did you watch *The Big Lebowski*? Come on, woman! You are taking forever to get back to me.

Obsessed Danielle

AUNT JOYCE E-MAIL 5/9
E-mail from Cool Aunt Joyce

Danielle,

Yes. Saw it. Loved it. Will take you to Lebowski Fest. Start planning your costumes. I'll have them made for you two. I will be going as a White Russian. We have a little time so you can obsess over your choice. I know you will.

Your Forever Aunt Joyce

DANIEL E-MAIL 5/10
E-mail I write to Daniel on my laptop after I finish my economics test early

My economics teacher is an *unapologetic* capitalist. I am not amused. We took a test today on the benefits of a market economy—quite frankly, the whole idea eludes me, and I'm not even sure I think a market economy or capitalism is a good idea—but anyway, there were advertisements for clothing stores and soft drinks on the test. I thought maybe I was supposed to use them in some answer or write about them in some way so I asked him about them. He said they were there because he had entered into a contract with those companies to advertise on his tests. WTF?

I have to admit that I started getting thirsty during the test and wanted a soda, which is just bullshit and shows how soft my mind is. I know teachers aren't paid what they deserve, but making money from tests by trying to sell us crap we don't need is bullshit. I think I just have to write off Mr. Richardson, and I kinda thought he was cool. Please advise.

DANIEL E-MAIL 5/10

Daniel writes back to me from his phone but he gets suspended because of it, which makes me feel super guilty.

That guy is completely unDude. You have to write him off. Do you know the slope formula, by chance?

ME-MOIR JOURNAL 5/15

My descent into sin, debauchery, and illegal activity. I swear I won't do this again, but I must admit the road to hell was paved with more fun than I anticipated.

   It is with deep regret that I report the first part of this journal entry because I got Daniel, my only friend, in trouble at school because I e-mailed him about my consumerist, *opportunistic* economics teacher and he responded (as friends are required to do), but then he asked me about the stupid slope formula, which isn't relevant to life except that life is one big slippery slope, and then he got suspended for cheating and using his phone in class. Arrrrggg! I didn't even know the damn slope formula, so I don't see this as technically cheating because there was no payoff, but "intent" is key here, as his administrators put it.

Daniel said he would just deal, which is the only thing to do in these cases. But then he said he wanted to get stoned, something he had never done before, which sort of surprised me and then made me happy.

I had never been officially stoned and I got all excited, which shocked me, when he proposed the idea. The only problem was that he had no idea how to get any weed and he didn't think I would know either because, just like him, I wasn't very "connected" at school. But Daniel was happy to learn that I did know where to get some! I told him about my neighbor whom my parents hated. I couldn't believe I was going to be a part of something so distasteful to my parents. They really had done nothing in my entire eighteen years on this planet to deserve what I was going to do, and I totally know I've already caused them plenty of trouble. They deserved a child much better than me. Nonetheless, I still told Daniel exactly where Ken (the corporate exec–looking guy with the twenty-two-year-old woman) lived, and let him figure out how to score; he said he'd do it, no problem. And he did! He wanted to tell me the whole story of how it all went down with Ken, but I started to have an anxiety attack during his retelling so he had to stop.

Friday night I went over to Daniel's. My parents were so thrilled that I continued to have "positive" social experiences on the weekend. (Little did they know. . . .)

Daniel's house was empty except for us, and all the baggage we carried that was, for one night, dropped. We unloaded so much on each other in just a few hours. Every conversation seemed pulled from an overstuffed piece of luggage; it took all night to unpack.

Daniel had a guitar in his room, which was just one instrument amid a sea of wires and music gear. Posters of musicians he loved decorated his walls, people like Jimi Hendrix and Bob Dylan. I didn't know Daniel was a musician. He said he hadn't played much lately but thinks he probably should again. He lit the joint as we sat cross-legged on the carpet in his bedroom while he let the guitar lay across his lap. When he was about ten, his real father turned him on to classic rock, and he taught himself the guitar. It was just something *innate* he could do; it made sense to him. That bewilders me, but he said the language of music is something some people are just born with. He was one of those people. Emily was, too.

After we took our first hit, he started talking about how he got asked to play his guitar and sing a song at his friend's bar mitzvah. That first hit of pot didn't seem to do anything to either of us. Daniel kept talking. He said I knew this friend Joel Stein, that he was in our class at Jefferson Middle School—I vaguely remembered the name when he said it, but that memory made me a little queasy, so I didn't think about it too much.

Joel's family admired how well he played the guitar and wanted him to pick a special song and sing it for all the guests. Daniel was really excited; he said, at the time, he wasn't a weirdo or a social outcast, and he loved to perform in front of people. He practiced for months and couldn't wait for the big day. His mom bought him his first suit.

At the bar mitzvah party, after the ceremony, Joel's father introduced Daniel, and he got up onstage to play and sing. No one had asked Daniel what he was playing. He said he played a flawless and inspired version of "Peace Train" by Cat Stevens, but before he could finish the song, he came out of his performer's trance and realized the crowd was not with him, people were uncomfortable and Joel's father was coming onstage to stop the performance. The song was not acceptable somehow, but Daniel didn't get it.

Joel's dad explained to him that Cat Stevens had become a Muslim with a new Muslim name and such songs were not to be played at a bar mitzvah. He still didn't understand. Jews are Jews and Muslims are Muslims. What did that have to do with the song he was playing for his friend? It was about peace. What's the big deal? How had he ruined the party? He didn't know the Jews and the Muslims were at odds so completely. The adults in the room were not amused at all by his song or his lack of awareness. Daniel thinks they believed he chose it on purpose to dishonor their sacred day. He felt like a *cad*.

Thank God Joel had perspective and humor even at thirteen. As Daniel was being ushered from the room, Joel got a chance to whisper in his ear—"I loved it, man. You just gotta know Cat Stevens is Jew repellant."

I couldn't stop laughing. At that moment, that was the funniest story I'd ever heard. I didn't know if I could hear the sound track to *Harold and Maude* the same way ever again. Daniel said he was afraid that he too would be Jew repellent, that all his Jewish friends from school would never speak to him again. It didn't happen, but he always felt a deep sense of shame for how clueless he was to the ways of the world.

I asked him then if he thought that was the incident that made him struggle in society, that ultimately led him to be a part of our illustrious social skills class.

"Oh, that such a single and innocent faux pas was the thing that derailed my 'peace train' from the tracks of life. Oh no, I kept making moves in the very wrong direction. It was like my life was being driven by a sadistic conductor who couldn't wait until I jumped the track. My demise was pretty much inevitable," he said. His eyes looked a little red at this point, like eyes do after a long cry. I wondered how mine looked.

Daniel kept talking. "I'm sure you know, Danielle, even though you've never said anything, I'm just sure you know: I'm gay."

I did know. I really did know. It had never really come up in conversation before or settled deep in my consciousness, but it was something I knew. I just didn't care at all. It's something to recognize that such a big thing about a person's identity had slipped my focus. I loved Daniel. I just knew I didn't love him in that way, and I guess I was so grateful because "that way" had shattered me. Daniel glued me back together. However he was going to be was fine with me. I loved our friendship, the thing it was, so the kind of love it was didn't matter to me. I was just grateful. I tried to tell Daniel all that I just wrote here, but it didn't come out that smoothly. I was a little loopy in my delivery. I ended my explanation to him with, "Wow, does this mean I'm finally somebody's fag hag?"

Daniel laughed and then added so charmingly, "No, my dear, you are my first fruit fly!"

Jew repellent, fruit fly, it was such an unplanned combination of insect imagery that I was filled with hilarity. I did a huge spit-take of the diet Coke I was drinking all over Daniel's down comforter, and we laughed until I nearly pissed myself. I am just so excited to be Daniel's fruit fly. It's so much better than being some straight guy's bitch! I said that out loud and we laughed some more.

Daniel said it is not being gay that destined his life to derail. He's fine with being gay. I said he was lucky because I wasn't so happy with being heterosexual—it wasn't doing me any favors! The problem with him is that he is forever falling in love with the straightest men on the planet—twisted Fate, was his phrase.

I was really lucky I could hide my feelings for Jacob because it is a dangerous world when this kind of love takes over. In class, Daniel would stare at Pete the quarterback, Perfect Pete the quarterback, Precious Pete the quarterback, delicious Pop-Tart Pete the quarterback. (I think we might have been really stoned by this point because there were more names given—Pet Pete the quarterback, Prowling Pete the quarterback, Pumped Pete the quarterback.)

Anyway, Pete was a magnet for Daniel's eyes in school. Sometimes it was literally minutes before Daniel realized he was staring at beautiful Pete. Staring at Pete too often is what got Daniel shoved up against the locker and a bloody nose. Daniel doesn't even blame Pete for doing that. "I was, like, stalking him with my eyes."

We each took another hit of pot. I think that was the third hit. Daniel kept going right after the deliberate exhale. (I think we did a really good job of smoking a joint. We looked just like kids do in the movies, all huddled by a bedside in an empty house spewing all our teen-aged crap.)

"I wrote a song after that incident at school. I'll play it for you." He played it for me, and I loved it. It's funny and and folksy and even though I'm a girl and the song is about a guy, I can totally relate to it. I hope Daniel records the song someday and other people can hear it, too, and I can listen to it whenever I want. It's called "Dumb Guy," and it's about being too young to be feeling so old and having regrets already.

I told him how awesome his song was, but I could tell Daniel was in an obsessive-thought mode, which I know super well so I didn't judge him or attempt to get him out of it. I just listened while he ranted.

"Goddammit, couldn't just one of my lusts be gay, too? Couldn't I be attracted to someone remotely genetically wired to be attracted to me? Otherwise, this problem is going to get me killed. Seriously, that conductor is trying to derail my fucking train! God, I'm such a fuckin' dumb guy!" Daniel screamed.

After he was done, I asked him, "Do your parents know you're gay?"

"Well, after I came home dented and bloodied from the locker incident, my stepdad asked what happened, and I said I had gotten beaten up for being a faggot. He didn't really react. My mom didn't really talk to me about it, but that is right around when I had to go to a Catholic church and when my mom signed me up for social skills class. I've never really come out to anyone formally except you. Tonight was the first time I uttered the words genuinely and with someone I trust. Yeah, wow, that was really something."

"Daniel, I know you're gay and all, and maybe if I wasn't stoned, I wouldn't say this—but, I really want to kiss you. I want to put my lips right on yours and try that out. One derailed train locked into another."

"Right about now, that sounds perfect."

And then I added, "But, would you mind if I pretended you were Jake Gyllenhaal?"

"Would you mind if I did?" he asked.

And there, stoned and alive and in the moment, I had my first real kiss from someone who knew me and loved me and was gay and didn't mind that I pretended he was Jake Gyllenhaal. It was so nice. I felt like it was the beginning of charting a new course. I think Daniel felt that way, too, because he yelled out "Damn girl!" and we fell on the floor laughing and laughed ourselves right to sleep.

JUSTINE LETTER

Dear Justine,
   Since we last communicated, my best friend came out to me (that means he told me he was gay) and, in English class, I have to try to write about how I stand out. All the ways that I can think of are embarrassing. You don't know me very well, but do you have any ideas? Thanks for being my friend.
   Sincerely,
   Danielle

ME-MOIR JOURNAL 5/20
Daniel and I plan our Lebowski outfits.

So Daniel and I had to watch *The Big Lebowski* more times to come up with the perfect Lebowski-fest outfit. He said it was key that we find something super nuanced that no one will ever wear. We spent time online looking up past costumes. All the characters are out. Everybody does that even though some people do it really creatively, like men come as Bunny, dressed in bikinis with green toenail polish. Also out is the rug that Woo pees on, "the queen in her damned undies"—although that is really funny—and other abstract props like the Port Huron Statement, Cynthia's dog's papers, or a cash machine.

I thought there was no way we were gonna find anything. Then I had a stroke of genius when we got to the end of the film. When the mortuary guy wants $180 for an urn for Donny's ashes, Walter yells: "Just because we're bereaved doesn't make us saps!" I said, "Let's go as bereaved people who aren't saps!"

Daniel wondered how we were gonna do that, but I said my fashion designing aunt would figure it out for sure. "After all," I told him, "that's exactly what we are in life—bereaved, but not saps." Despite what any quarterback or *moo*ing asshole thought.

✳MARV MISSIVE✳
Letter from me to Marv about an unfortunate event during "Spirit Week"

Marv,

Could you please explain to me why James got suspended for the outfit he wore today for Decade Day? (I dressed like the sixties in a tie-dyed shirt and painted a peace symbol on my face in case you didn't see me today.) Anyway, look, the eighteen hundreds had decades and so why did James get in trouble for dressing like a slave? There were slaves in many decades in the eighteen hundreds. The shackles he wore had to be pretty expensive, and those whip marks took some effort to create. I applaud his effort. If we were only allowed to dress in outfits from the nineteen sixties, seventies, or eighties, someone should have told us. I know the administration told James his outfit was inappropriate, and he responded by saying, "Yeah, it is pretty frickin' inappropriate. It was inappropriate for hundreds of years." James was right. So why was he suspended?

Confused,
Danielle

MARV MISSIVE
Letter from Marv to me, which I receive soon after my letter to him.

Danielle,
I have two explanations for you. One, people may have believed he was mocking a terrible situation. Or, two, in the face of undeniable, painful truth, many do not know how to react. They just want it to go away.

Marv

MARV MISSIVE
Letter from me to Marv

Marv,
  Thank you.
  Danielle

ME-MOIR JOURNAL 5/26
We have dinner with the social skills class and
an unfortunate thing happens.

The quest to get my mother to see that I am now beyond
my social skills class continues. I'm done. I've got a friend.
Daniel keeps playing the same card with his parents, too, and
they aren't biting either. He even tried to tell them he has a
newfound relationship with the Lord and that should suffice.
They don't agree.

So we were both stuck going to dinner with the class at the
Galleria on a Saturday night, which is just death. The entire
Meadow Oaks student body goes to the Galleria on Saturday. My mom said that would be wonderful because people
would see me socializing. Oh God, she just never gets it. But
Daniel and I realized we would have to go. He suggested we
get stoned beforehand because we had one joint left. I didn't
want to do that. It's one thing to do that alone in his room. I
didn't trust myself out in public that way. Although, looking

back on how I actually behaved, I would have been better off stoned.

Anyway, we met at the restaurant. You couldn't miss Lisa, who was wearing the brightest yellow suit I'd ever seen. She looked like a banana. Does she own anything but these suits? I wore my green sherpa hat even though the weather is warm because I thought, worse case scenario, if I didn't want to listen to anybody, I could tie the flaps over my ears.

We all looked like we were taken out of the asylum for a night, which was kind of true. We were sitting as a befuddled, geeky group at a big table in the front of the restaurant when Jacob, Keira, James, and Heather walked through the door. I saw Keira see me and move her group toward our table for at least a "hello" and at worst a public shaming.

I reacted totally on crazed instinct. Daniel was seated next to me, and I leaned over and grabbed his face and planted a big kiss on him as Keira and Jacob approached the table. Daniel was stunned but recovered quickly when he realized who was standing before us.

"Hey, Danielle," Keira said. "Is this your boyfriend?"

In quite deliberate language I said, "Yes, Keira, this is my boyfriend, Daniel. And Daniel this is Jacob."

"Hey, man," Jacob condescended.

Daniel brilliantly continued, "Hey, are you guys joining our Save the Children dinner meeting? We can pull up chairs."

Lisa was stunned. She had no idea what was going on, and all the other doofuses just stared in disbelief that I had kissed

Daniel so boldly. Iggie threw some paper bird in the air and slammed his head down on the table. So weird.

Jacob said, "Naw, we're here to eat before we see a movie. But you guys have fun saving the planet. Later, Danielle."

After they left, Lisa lectured everyone on the poor social graces of lying about yourself out in public. "You all have nothing to be ashamed of, so covering up who you are to impress others is not necessary. Now I expect all of us to think about what we can actually do to begin to save the children in order to live up to the lie that Daniel has set forth tonight."

"Well, then I'd say my lie was a good thing. Getting this group to do something other than whine about our circumstances can only be good. I, for one, think we should shift the entire social skills class into a Save the Children group. All in favor?" Every hand shot up.

Mission accomplished.

Daniel did talk to me about not using him to make myself look better to Jacob, even though he did agree to go to my prom with me because he could masquerade as a full-fledged straight guy and stare at all the boys without fear of fists. He couldn't see what I saw in Jacob, actually. I thought for sure Daniel would take one look at him and fall in love.

"No. If I know up front he's straight but an asshole, the asshole trumps straight, and I'm immediately turned off. Generally, I have to discover them on my own, like them first, think they are dreamy and perfect and smell good, and then I find out they are jerks, get my face smashed into a locker or some metaphorical equivalent, and then get over them. You took the locker to the face for me on this one. He's got a little prick—you can tell."

"OMG, really?"

"Totally."

JUSTINE LETTER

Dear Danielle,

How nice your friend is gay. That's just fine by me. As far as how you stand out, just know everyone stands out. Each life is a unique blend of energy that colors the planet. Think about the energy that is you, that you give off. Where did that energy come from? What has happened in your life that gave you your unique <u>you</u> quality. Pick one little or big thing, it doesn't matter. If you are honest, how you stand out will read loud and clear like the crisp air in the morning of a new day. In your essay, just be who you are. I, for one, like her very much.

Do you know what I do each week, Danielle? I mean besides my tours. Each week, I meet with five other women I've known now for over thirty years, my goodness. When we first started meeting, we were all grieving widows. We did a lot of boohooing together for a while. But, you know what, we needed to be that for a little bit. That was who we were.

And then one day, one of the women started talking about a lusty romance novel she was reading. Oh my. We couldn't help ourselves, Danielle. We all went home and bought that book. Since then, our grieving widows group has become a romance book club. Are you picturing that, dear? Five old ladies sitting in a pub snickering over silly books, talking all about the impossible lives of fictional people? Well, that's what we do, my dear, because our youthful shame and guilt left us long ago. We do that and we make meals with each other and we go to church and we live.

> Good-bye for now, dear,
> Justine

AUNT JOYCE AND DANIEL E-MAIL 5/27
E-mail from me to Daniel (late so I couldn't call) with a cc to Aunt Joyce

So, my aunt sent drawings of the costumes she's having made for us! I've cc'd her on this e-mail so you can write her back with your shirt size, shoe size, and pant size. Daniel, you're gonna love the getup! Thank you, Aunt Joyce, you save us.

ME-MOIR JOURNAL 5/30
Daniel drags me to confession

Daniel has been trying for weeks to get me to go to confession with him. I have not been inclined. However, Daniel reminded me that he agreed to be my "straight" date for the prom, that I had used him to make Jacob think that I had a boyfriend, and that I was his friend, and he just wanted me to go with him. Heaven help me, literally. Catholic churches weird me out.

At this particular church, a huge Jesus hangs on a cross front and center. You can't miss it. There are statues everywhere of people weeping and falling to their knees, and all this creepy decor that is outside my comfort zone. The place needs my mom to come in and happy it up a little.

Daniel told me what to do. I had to get in that sin-box and start by saying, "Bless me, father, for I have sinned. It's been (fill in time period) since my last confession, and these are my sins." I didn't know what I'd list as my sins, but I planned to improvise. We had to kneel down for a while first. I was supposed to pray. I didn't really know what to do, so I just closed my eyes and let my mind go blank. When an elderly woman carrying what Daniel told me was a rosary exited the sin-box, he told me to go in. I did. It was claustrophobic. I guess the appropriate environment for a sinner, one of God's wayward children. Sinners need containing. The priest on the other side of the box slid a little door to reveal a screen like a fast-food worker at a drive-through. I said my line and the performance began. After an interminable silence, the priest said, "Begin, my child."

I don't know where this came from, but I said, "I'm a fraud." The priest wanted me to explain. I said, "There is no explanation. I am just a fraud. I hide out. I hide from the truth."

"And what is the truth?" he asked.

I report these facts:

"I lost my friend. I turned off the faucet in my brain that controls all her liquid memories. I pretend that a flood of truth doesn't exist. I loved a boy who didn't love me. I pretend like that's fine. I violated my parents' trust. I don't tell them all the ways I've done that. I'm pretending a gay boy is my boyfriend so people think I'm loved. I take comfort in pretending to be like everyone else even though I know I never will be. I'm a disappointment as a human being."

The priest was not a big talker; he got straight to his point: "You are not a disappointment as a human being," he said. "That would be impossible. You, young lady, are part of the one body of Christ. The Lord does not see with the same eyes we do. Your life is a gift as it is. Say four Hail Marys and an Our Father. Good night, young lady."

Wow. Well, I guess I could see the appeal of this religion. You can be a giant fraud and make it all better with a few chants.

When Daniel finished his thing in the sin-box, he ran over to me, that's right, ran over to me, in a place I was sure no running was allowed, as I pretended to pray the chants the priest told me to. He grabbed my hand and said, "We gotta get the hell outta here." I know Daniel won't admit this, but I could tell he had been crying.

On the street, he explained that he couldn't act appropriately in the confessional. I'm not exactly sure what he meant by that, but he kept saying it . . . that he couldn't act appropriately in there. He said he needed to do more reading about how our psychology influences our actions, so he could understand himself better.

Anyway, this time when he got in the enclosed dark box, he started looking around and breathing in the sawdust smell and just settling into the darkness. He said something "primal" possessed him. Suddenly, he just really wanted to connect with the guy on the other side of the drive-through window. He wanted to know who he was, he wanted to "psychologically reach across that veil" is how Daniel put it.

Instead of confessing made-up sins, he started asking the priest genuine questions about his life. Like how old he was, how long was he a priest, did he like it? What was the best part of priesthood? He and the priest started having a conversation. Daniel said, "I felt like I was starting to get to know the guy or something."

I said, "Well, that's cool, right?"

"I don't know. That hadn't been my goal. I mean, it wasn't sexy or rebellious or sacrilegious or any of the things that I come here for. It was just human. I was just talking to the guy."

"Wow. Maybe Lisa and the social skills class is helping you connect with people in a more real way or something."

Big pause.

"Holy crap. Take that back right now, Danielle. That is just the devil talking right through you."

"What? I'm just saying it's possible."

"No. That woman has done no good for me whatsoever. Her purpose in my life is for her to be the receiver of my witty mockery. She is mere entertainment. I gotta go. I'm going home to rub one out, so I can forget about what you said about Lisa. Danielle, seriously, that is so disturbing."

Daniel went home and who knows what he did or if it was a success. LOL. He called me later and asked if I'd come over and have dinner with him. I did.

We wrote a song together about angels, even though we are a couple of devils. It won't translate properly if I add it to my writing collection because I can't make a page sing or strum a guitar. But if I could, Daniel's talent would be evident. He plucks a guitar with the kind of tenderness that a man should give a woman or a man should give a man (in Daniel's case).

(Everyone in my class was forced to write this essay
because Ms. Harrison wanted us to see ourselves in a
powerful light before college or something.)

Danielle Levine
English 12
Ms. Harrison
Period 4

What makes me stand out is all that I have had to abide. I
know my peers are aware of a certain ugliness that defines me,
and because of that, I am nervous to read this essay aloud.
They know my ugliness, but they don't know how I came to
be this way. I have created a separation from my classmates
to save them and me from the truth. However, there is no
barrier strong enough to protect you from life. It finds you.
Friends come even if you are not looking for them. Loss finds
you even if you aren't ready.

I met my best friend, Emily, in the second grade when her
family moved in next door to us in Orange County. We dug a
hole under the fence that separated our yards, and we slid back
and forth daily into each other's domains even when we were
supposed to be doing homework or folding our laundry. We
were yelled at many times for how dirty our school clothes got

when we forgot to change before we rolled around in the dirt. We played lifeguards, store owners, cheerleaders, waitresses, rock stars—I sang into a vacuum sweeper and flung the cord around with verve while Emily played her oboe.

I've never met anyone else in my life who played the oboe. And she played it so well at such a young age. She was a child prodigy, truly. It used to make me mad that she had this talent. I said bad things I regret now because I was jealous of that oboe, which got more of her time than me, I used to think. Her talent brought out the worst in me and, for that, I have deep regret.

But on the weekends, she still found all the time we needed to jump on the trampoline she had and swim in the pool that I had. We had sleepovers all the time. We had this friendship together, we had all this, until we were in eighth grade.

One night during an eighth-grade sleepover at her house, we pretended to sleep under Emily's juvenile Dora the Explorer sheets until her parents fell asleep. We were excited to sneak out and go "crap shopping," as we called it, at the convenience store not far from our houses. We wanted Sour Patch Kids and Red Vines with a large Coke (to dip the Red Vines in), and all the fixings for s'mores. We planned to devour it all under the sheets with flashlights, like we were on a camping adventure.

It took forever for her parents to settle so they were asleep enough to not know we were gone; we didn't leave until midnight. Equipped with flashlights, stuffed animals, and a camera to capture our adventure on film, we walked into the store.

Minutes later, with our treats overflowing in our hands, we were in line to pay. I looked over at the entrance when the door opened and a bell rang. A man in military fatigues walked in brandishing a weapon (an assault rifle, I later heard someone say). He was shouting orders to who knows who. He ducked around the magazine rack and kept shouting. He was yelling coordinates that meant something to him, and he seemed really afraid, but I, to this day, have no idea of what.

Emily dropped all the candy she was holding, and I don't know why, it was an instinct, I guess, but I dropped down and tried to gather up the candy. As soon as I dropped down, the gunman peeked around the corner and aimed his rifle right at Emily and opened fire. *Pow. Pow. Pow.* Emily's camera clicked, clicked, clicked because her finger was on it when she was shot. Her final view of life was captured in those pictures, freeze-framed horrors, emblazoned forever on film.

Her last photograph, the one she snapped as she turned and looked in my direction before she fell to the bloody ground, was of me. I saw the picture because her mother couldn't destroy any of them, couldn't let them go, even though they are horrible and disturbing. She can't let go of the symbols of her daughter's last moments on Earth. I wish she could have destroyed that picture of me because it is a shameful snapshot, an indictment of my helplessness. It is the ugliest picture I have ever seen. I was caught on film living.

I forgive Emily's mom for keeping all the pictures, though, because they are something tangible to cling to, some way to hold on to a life she loved. I understood because for weeks after that night, I couldn't stop wandering into the convenience store and lying down on the exact spot where Emily died, near the spot where I had done nothing but stare. I didn't care who was in the store at these times. I pushed people out of line and lay down and tried to hug the tile floor. I rubbed my face all over the dirty floor. I tried to swallow the smell and the taste of that floor. I did it every day even when adults tried to keep an eye on me; I eluded their care. I kept doing it even when the owner would call the police and have me carried out. Her life was poured all over that floor.

Being shot isn't like it is in the movies. There isn't a little hole in the body and a few slow trickles of blood that allow for surprise in the victim's eyes and time to say final, profound words. No. Bullets rip and tear through flesh in an instant; blood gushes through a wound and floods an area. I had no idea a human held so much blood. I would lay on the floor and see that blood as it was in that moment and try to gather it up in my hands wishing I had thought quicker and tried to funnel that life back into her when I had the chance. Why didn't I?

Every day I cut school the second I could and headed back to the floor of that store. I grabbed a broom one day and tried to sweep the mirage of blood I was sure was there. I tried to sweep it into a puddle and then scoop it back into her imagined body.

My parents did the absolute best they could for me during this time, but I was beyond help. They did the only thing they could. We moved from Orange County to the Valley in Los Angeles, and I started Meadow Oaks in ninth grade, and now you all know why. I was supposed to start a new life, too, but the same old tortured me had come along.

I've had a very hard time understanding my tortured self, but some things have occurred this year that have helped me. One of those helping moments came when we were reading the scene in *Hamlet* when Laertes sees his crazy sister, Ophelia, for the first time and says, "Nature is fine in love and where 'tis fine, it sends some precious instance of itself after the thing it loves." That is exactly what happened to me. As Emily's blood drained out of her, a piece of me was draining out, too.

Nature *IS* fine in love, fine, as in *thin* and *delicate*, as in *not firm*. We move to attach, more than we understand, to things and people we love that we feel might be an anchoring point for this fine, precious love. When those anchors disappear, a part of us disappears, too. Well, that's how it was for me at least.

There must be a better way to love and to live, a way to be a lover of things without attaching. I don't know exactly what that new way is yet, but when I go to college, I hope I will read more things written by smarter people than me who give me some insight into this condition. Somewhere within some kind of art must be a message worth clinging to about all these things we have to endure because of all these attachments.

While my circumstances make me stand out, paradoxically,

they are what make me just like everyone else. Everyone has things that they must abide.

Comments from Ms. Harrison: *There is not a thing I can say.* **A**

POEM

Emily Brontë wrote, "Any relic of the dead is precious, if they were valued living." After I read that last essay aloud in class, I went home and started going through all the papers in the back of my closet. I found this poem crumpled in a box with a friendship bracelet that is a match to one Emily had and a picture of me and Emily with her oboe. I wrote the following poem after Emily died.

> I haven't laughed in so damn long,
> I don't know what's wrong.
> Memories of tragedies belong
> In a made-up song,
> And I'm trying not to weep
> Like a child who's fallen down and skinned her knee
> I haven't moved from this cold chair,
> Comfortable despair.
> Dreams that dance around perchance to care
> Can't find me anywhere,

And I'm trying to perceive

My superhero's innate joie de vivre.

So defend your world until its bitter end

And let all things that pass be born again.

You see, my friend, it's not like God not to mend.

We do not die, we cannot stop

The bittersweet teardrop.

Evidence of confidence in this

Is easy to miss, so easy to miss,

And I know I must believe

Like a child who's half asleep on Christmas Eve.

ME-MOIR JOURNAL 6/5
Candle Lighting

Meadow Oaks has a ceremony every year that I've always been both nervous and excited to be a part of during my senior year. Candle Lighting is where the torch of leadership is passed from the senior class to the junior class. (I don't know how this senior class has demonstrated any leadership whatsoever, but we still got to have the ceremony.) Each senior pairs up with a junior and walks down the aisle together in the auditorium that is tastefully decorated with dim lights and flower arrangements. The senior lights a candle and then lights a junior's candle. It's pretty cool. But the coolest part is what happens before that. Ms. Harrison, who is the senior adviser, roasts every senior. She writes funny, but somehow loving, tribute roasts for each one of us. She reads it to the crowd while the roastee stands front and center to be "mocked."

I was sure I'd be an easy target for any roast. I didn't imagine Ms. Harrison could find any loving words to describe me, but I was wrong. We each got a copy of our roasts so I can write mine here in this journal. This is what Ms. Harrison said about me:

"Danielle Levine stands out whether she knows it or not, whether she wants to or not. She italicizes all the vocabulary words in her essays as if I am too dense to know I taught her those words. Danielle stands out as a writer despite her stubborn stance against my guidelines, against a formal voice, against standard sentence structure in essay writing. But, from Danielle, I've learned that minds that learn differently teach others to see things differently. Also, I've learned the importance of reading an even number of pages in class to feed the beast that is OCD. Danielle is a liberator of sorts, as well. Thank you for bravely releasing my bandaged tattoo through civil disobedience. Mr. Resurrection can be proud that you incorporated his history lessons so well. May you, too, find liberation by similar methods throughout your life."

Ms. Harrison is so smart and nice. She made me feel special not in a special-ed way but in a human way.

I made a point of remembering Jacob's roast which began, "Jacob Kingston prowls around campus like the king of the jungle. His beastly persona breaks hearts and windows. We know you were the one who lobbed a rock through Mr. Chin's chemistry lab window, but were too prideful to own your mistake. However, your parents already have because the school sent them a bill!"

Nice work, Ms. Harrison. I didn't realize she knew what a heartbreaker Jacob is. She made other references to classmate's behavior that I thought was deeply hidden amid teenage *subterfuge*, but no, Ms. Harrison was aware. She was hip to much more than I knew. Will wonders never cease?

Daniel came to Candle Lighting with my parents and Aunt Joyce. They loved it and all said they were proud of me for "my showing in the event." My parents and Aunt Joyce drove together and, after giving me bigs hugs, said they'd see Daniel and me back at the house where we could try on our Lebowski Fest outfits that Joyce had with her. After they left and the crowd was thinning, Daniel and I were still talking at the back of the auditorium when Jacob came up to us. He said to me, "Danielle, you really are a great writer. I always like listening to the essays you read in class. That last one, the one about your friend, was that true?"

Daniel kissed my cheek and excused himself by saying, "Hey, babe, I'll drive the car around and meet you in the parking lot." (OMG but Daniel is the best pretend boyfriend ever.)

I didn't know how to answer Jacob's question. Of course that essay was true. It didn't dawn on me that anyone would think it wasn't. It was so difficult for me to read that essay out loud, but when I did, it was such a relief to get it out of me. I felt myself move into myself further, literally, as if I had been,

207

for years, a cartoon drawn by a drunk, cross-eyed artist who couldn't keep me in the lines. I lived outside myself, just barely overlapping my skin and bones until that moment when I just told the truth about who I was as simply as I could manage. I assumed everyone could see the relief and the truth of it and now know the main reason that I was such a freak. I assumed that was why nobody said much to me about it; they wanted to leave me alone while I took time to fully process my freakdom.

I stared at Jacob and he continued, "Well, because if it isn't true, you really are an amazing storyteller. That whole situation was just wack. A bunch of us have been talking about it. You should study writing or something."

"Okay. Thanks, Jacob," was all I could say. Jacob Kingston couldn't see me at all.

When I got in the car, I talked to Daniel about the whole thing. Daniel said Jacob couldn't see me because he is a native.

I didn't know what Daniel meant. He said he heard this story that he wasn't sure was actually true, but he liked it anyway because it has a good lesson. He said that a long time ago Spanish ships carrying conquistadors were coming over the horizon on their way to overtake indigenous people, and the natives onshore did nothing to prepare for the attack because they literally couldn't see the ships.

"So, I'm a conquistador in this analogy?" I asked.

"Just be quiet and listen to me," he said.

Daniel went on to say the natives had no point of reference to even be able to process what a ship was, so they couldn't see it. We can't see what we don't know was Daniel's point.

"But why does Jacob get to be an innocent native, and I have to be a vicious conquistador?"

"Would you stop being so rigid in your thinking! I'm just saying that he doesn't have the proper frame of reference to see the truth of who you are. No one is a conquistador in this scenario!"

"Oh, good. But, I do like the natives, though."

"Sheesh, Danielle. I'm trying to teach you something. Also, you are not a freak because of that event in your life. That's not the only thing that defines you. You're a freak for a whole lot of other reasons."

"Good one."

"Hey, by the way, what did Jacob write about for that essay?"

"Exactly what you'd think," I told him.

"Did he write about football?"

"Damn right. He wrote about being the quarterback."

"Of course he did. I hate those fuckers."

When we got home, we tried on our costumes for Lebowski Fest. We loved them. Also, as a huge surprise, Aunt Joyce bought our prom outfits from a designer friend of hers. My dress was a gorgeous emerald green off the shoulder (which made me nervous, but Joyce, just like Daniel, told me to shut up). Daniel's suit had a emerald green shirt and tie, which was way cooler than a cummerbund match, according to my aunt. She also bought us matching diamond earrings. (Well, just one for Daniel. Joyce said he was completely sexy enough to pull off the one earring and still appear straight if that was his wish . . . although, he would definitely turn the heads of the gay boys, too. I agreed!) This is a miracle to report but: I can't wait for the prom.

MARV MISSIVE
Letter from Marv to me

Danielle,

I won't lie to you. I've been speaking with your mother and your social skills leader, Lisa. Both report that you seem happy, which is all any of us ever wanted for you. Is it true?
    Marv

MARV MISSIVE
Letter from me to Marv

Marv,

It really pisses me off that you would talk to Lisa and believe anything she says. Her behavior caused me to kiss my gay friend in public. Don't ask. Just know she's a mess. Besides that, yes, it's true, I am learning "to firm my inner smile," which is something my yoga teacher says. But I'm no fool. I know these feelings aren't lasting.
    Danielle

MARV MISSIVE
Letter from Marv to me

Danielle,

I didn't ask if you found lasting happiness, just happiness. Nothing is lasting, but I know you are aware of that as you prepare to graduate from high school. I am very proud of you. Also, your mother told me you are going to prom— bravo for you. Lisa is not as bad or as stupid as you think.

Marv

MISSED MARV MISSIVE
Letter I think to write to Marv but never actually give to him

Marv,

You have been a good help to me this year, although, I'm shocked to find myself thinking that. Sometimes your little notes kept me afloat on days I thought I'd drown. Still, I think you're wrong about Lisa.

Danielle

The month of June has several exciting events for me, and Lebowski Fest was the one I was looking forward to the most. We arrived an hour early after finding an In-N-Out Burger where I ordered the grilled cheese. We ate in the car and listened to the movie sound track to prep for the night. The Fest was in Carson at a bowling alley, and when we arrived, there were hundreds of costumed fanatics waiting in line to get in.

Joyce and Karen were big hits as White Russians because they are gorgeous and draw a crowd for that reason. One guy in line behind us was dressed as Bunny in nothing but a green bikini, blond wig, and green toenail polish, but he did not make a necessary waxing appointment before the event. He was a very hairy Bunny.

Daniel and I were wearing all black. I wore a dress with "Bereaved but not a Sap" embroidered on the pocket in white lettering. A wide-rimmed black hat with a veil covered my face (loved that). Daniel looked awesome in a black pinstriped suit with a cool gangster-style hat. He had the same embroidered words that I did on his lapel. We both had holsters and fake guns—we're not saps! There were Dudes everywhere representing the character at various points in the film. My favorites were the robe-wearing Dudes who managed to get those clear jelly sandals that are just hideous but look right on The Dude.

Daniel had a conversation with a guy dressed as Jackie Treehorn, the known pornographer in the film. In real life he was a surfing rabbi who was also a league bowler. He knew the owners of the Carson bowling alley and was scheduled to have a lane once we got in the place. We didn't think we'd actually be able to bowl because there were so many people, and it was difficult to get a lane. We were planning to just watch everything from the sidelines. But "Jackie" liked Aunt Joyce (no surprise), and so she flirted her way into an invitation to play on his lane. (Pun not intended. I am talking about literally bowling.) She didn't go out with him or anything, but he was normal enough, as normal as you can be while dressed as a known pornographer. When he invited us to play on his lane she said, "I like the way you do business, man," and Daniel and I were so happy that Aunt Joyce knew the movie enough to quote it like everyone else was doing all night.

To really enjoy this night, you had to be completely obsessed with the world of this movie so you could keep up and play your part. Daniel and I did just fine. We watched the movie about ten times so when The Eagles started playing over the loudspeaker we yelled right on cue with everyone else, "I hate the fuckin' Eagles, man!" just like The Dude.

In a weird alternative universe like Lebowski Fest, it's appropriate that bizarre things happen. Two bizarre things did happen (a good even number). One: I found out I was super good at bowling, even in an evening dress, and two: Iggie from social skills class was there with his two brothers who were dressed as nihilists and who were card-carrying, ordained

Dudeist priests. I have to say that I learned so much about Dudeism from these two because they talked about it all night as they bowled in the lane next to us.

To summarize, Dudeism is about "takin' 'er easy," which is what we were all doing at the bowling alley, so I guess we were in Dudeist church in the truest sense. These two listed a bunch of reasons for the benefits of just chillin', and while they probably didn't do very well in school, they seemed really happy. They recommended we check out the Church of the Latter-Day Dude online. I guess they liked to proselytize, which is something I learned about years ago when I let these seemingly nice men in black suits, white shirts, and black ties into our house, and we couldn't get rid of them. My father was furious with me. I think he wouldn't mind the way Iggie's brothers proselytized while they bowled and drank "oat sodas."

It was so weird that Iggie ended up at Lebowski Fest, bowling in a lane right next to us. He personified the movie line "I can get you a toe by three o'clock, with nail polish" and was wearing a huge papier-mâché clock set at three o'clock and carried a giant sack filled with papier-mâché baby toes, nails painted green. The toes looked great and the clock had so much detail, and I realized that all those paper things he folds in social skills class do reveal a very unique talent, and Iggie should probably just be left alone to do his art and find his place in the world that way and not be forced into becoming a more social creature. What if his talent gets lost in the socialization process? Maybe he's fine being a paper-art-genius hermit. Also, if he's at Lebowski Fest, how off could he really be? I had a new lease on Iggie!

And now, about my bowling: either I'm a closet bowling savant, or I just had a very lucky night. Maybe due to the blessings of the Dudeist priests present or the super-chill vibe of the night, but I bowled a ton of strikes, one right after another. I had to hike up my bereaved-but-not-a-sap dress a little in very unladylike fashion, but it made everyone laugh, and then I would just stare at the pins and roll the ball and watch all the pins smash to the ground. Maybe my extra weight was a plus in this sport. Is it a sport?

While the lane spirits smiled on me, they also smiled on Daniel. One of the Dudeist priests, Jonas, hit it off with Daniel. Between rolls they poured over *Big Lebowski* essays that Jonas had with him in a briefcase. He was very interested in the essay that Daniel helped me write relating to *King Lear*. Jonas said Daniel had to get *The Year's Work in Lebowski Studies* so the two of them could discuss it. Jonas would have loaned it to Daniel, but it made him nervous when the book was out of his care for too long. He said this book was one of the few things on the planet that was actually worth spending money for.

Toward the end of the night when it was Daniel's turn to bowl, Jonas went to the bathroom, and Daniel asked Iggie if Jonas had a girlfriend. Iggie didn't look up from adjusting some of the toes that had been tweaked in his bag when he said, "No, he's gay. He's totally into you."

Daniel dropped his bowling ball on his shoe.

I was going to tell him he could get a new toe from Iggie, but instead I told him that I thought he finally found a way to be legitimately molested by a priest. And I was really happy for him.

Daniel got Jonas's phone number before we all left. It was a really chill time.

CLASS ASSIGNMENT 6/12
Lessons from High School Friendships

(A-)

Danielle Levine
Ms. Harrison
English 12
Period 4

First off, Ms. Harrison, I want to tell you that I am off my Adderall tonight. I did not do this intentionally. My house-keeper accidentally knocked over the bottle containing my last three Adderall for this week and the pills went down the disposal and are gone forever and will take a day to replace. She felt really bad. I hope I managed to pay attention in class today but it was really hard, so I hope you'll forgive me if I was not what you expected. It is very hard for me to finish anything I start when I'm off my Adderall, so the completion of this essay will be a sheer act of will done in your honor.

Secondly, I know we have to make an allusion to another work of art in this essay (which is a rhetorical device you love and that I've come to appreciate because good art reflects life and a good life reflects art) and I hope you can soften something inside yourself and embrace the fact that I'm going to use a YouTube video as my selected art piece. (Softening something is what David, my yoga teacher, always asks us to do when we are in a hard pose for a long time, and I always think that this is a ridiculous request to make of me since my whole body is soft, but now that I am writing this to you I understand a different meaning for "soften something.")

If you had asked me to write an essay about high school friendships at the beginning of the year, I would have turned in something dismal that would have earned me a meeting with Marv, but now at the end of the year, I have a new perspective on the idea of high school friendships. And I'm going to tell you about it.

There is a YouTube video that you can find and should be called "Sassy Gay Friend: Hamlet." In it, Ophelia is poised to drown herself when her sassy gay friend leaps on the scene and says to her in a very funny way, "What, what, what are you doing?!" (That makes me really laugh.) Then he says, "O-feel-ya-so bad for yourself, move away from the water!" (That makes me laugh, too.) He continues, "Instead of drowning yourself you're gonna write a sad poem in your journal and MOVE ON!" (He says other funny things like "There IS something rotten in Denmark and it's [Hamlet's] piss-poor attitude!" (That is so true.) Anyway, by the end of the video, Ophelia is not going to kill herself and her sassy gay friend even tells her that her hair never looked better, and he couldn't believe she was going to get it wet.

I have been where Ophelia was. I've wanted to just drown! (Also, I had a friend leap onto the scene [metaphorically] and save me [literally], and although my friend is gay, he is not sassy, but this is not the salient point of my essay.) I wish Ophelia really did have someone to tell her all the things that the Ophelia in the YouTube video is told so that *Hamlet* could have ended differently. Sometimes you need another person to help you shift your perspective. (Also, the point about writing in her journal was excellent. I've written a sad poem before and that might have helped Ophelia, but she would have needed to be patient because healing takes time.) I am glad I hung in there until a genuine friend appeared for me. My life may not be a full-out tragedy from this point, and my friend Daniel is a big reason why.

So, nothing about high school was what I thought. Nothing about my friendships was what I thought either. I'm going to try to not have too many thoughts about the way I think things should be. That is what my high school friendships have taught me.

Surprising Comments from Ms. Harrison: *Once again, Danielle, I'm at a loss over how to grade you. This essay is not what I had in mind. However, I, too, have a close friend who* *has kept me from drowning and there is much truth in what you wrote.*

✳ME-MOIR JOURNAL✳ 6/19
Prom

Prom took place about a week before graduation. Daniel and I couldn't believe we were actually at a prom and had dates. If someone told me in September that I'd be standing here in June, I'd have told that person to go back on his meds.

Daniel said he was actually happy to pretend to be straight just to have a culturally acceptable, socially packaged experience in order to be able to write a song about it someday and to tell the child he one day adopts with his beautiful, rich, and well-endowed husband, that his one father had gone to a prom with a woman—just in case his child actually cared about that kind of thing. He didn't want to be the kind of dad that disappoints, he said.

I told Daniel I was not going to have children, and he said that would be a shame because I had such beautiful red hair and stunning green eyes and I should give those qualities a shot at continuing . . . not to mention the huge heart . . . which all made me cry and grab Daniel and actually take him on to the dance floor and dance.

I don't know what anyone thought of us. I don't know if people even talked about us; I didn't care at all. I didn't react anywhere in my mind or in my body when Keira and Jacob were crowned prom king and queen. They looked beautiful. Really. They had that kind of beauty that shows up in teenage movies and magazines. I could smell their freshness just by looking at them.

After the king and queen dance, Daniel grabbed my hand and we managed to sneak out through the kitchen, avoid chaperones, and make it to Daniel's car. He grabbed his guitar and something else and ushered me, breathless from running, behind the science building and under a tree with low hanging branches. It was dark, but the stars were many because the sky was so clear.

We sat down and Daniel pulled out the one remaining joint from our night of sin. "No! Daniel, we can't do that here. I can't."

"Come on, Danielle. Just to seal the deal. High school. Been there. Done that."

"Ahhhhh. Why do you do this to me?"

"Because you are my fruit fly."

"You snot. One hit."

And so he lit the joint, and we took turns inhaling and staring into each other's faces. I wonder if he thought the same thing I did—that I never imagined the face of my best friend would look like this. I never imagined any face after Emily's, but I surely couldn't have imagined his. Daniel has beautiful black hair, and he, too, has green eyes. They were piercing and cold, like frozen winter ponds, but they were the windows to the warmest soul I'd ever known. He was a gift from somewhere, from someone. Gay or straight, I love him, the way people are supposed to love.

"Sing me a song, Danielle. You really have a sexy voice."

"I do?"

"Yeah. Even your speaking voice is sexy as hell. It's all whispery and shit. Some man is going to go wild over it."

I smiled. A real, true woman's smile.

"Now start me a song, woman."

In my green, elegant dress that was now more wrinkled and dirtied than I should have ever let it become, with my foggy head that was higher than I should have ever let it become, I sang.

There was something about singing into the night air that made me feel powerful and safe. A space inside me expanded. Daniel's gorgeous guitar melody was so easy to feel, not just hear, and words kept coming out of me. I imagined them floating all the way up to the sky. In my mind's eye, without trying, I saw Emily hear them, and strangely, I swear, I could hear the soft sounds of an oboe.

When our impromptu song ended, and the air was still cool and crisp and smelled of greenery, Daniel pulled out the joint one more time, but as he lit it, Ms. Harrison walked around the side of the building and stood above us. Something about the way she was there, about the way she moved in the darkness, made me feel like she had been standing there for a while.

I panicked inside and my heart beat wildly. Daniel quickly

hid the joint behind his back in a futile attempt to save us and grabbed my hand as if to silence my heart. We both stared at my favorite teacher.

Calmly, but with purpose, Ms. Harrison said, "I want you two to get up, go back inside, and do not leave the prom until I give you permission to go. This evening's festivities are to be enjoyed inside."

I breathed an audible sigh of relief and choked back tears that had been building. Maybe Ms. Harrison wasn't doing the right thing according to the school, but I was so grateful for her response. In my mind I said to her, I'll never smoke pot again. I swear. Thank you for pretending like you don't know what we were doing. Thank you.

Back inside, Daniel and I danced for a while, and then we talked to Marv. Daniel really liked him, like thought he was handsome, that kind of like. I told Daniel that Marv is an older guy whose business it is to probe into people's psyches, and I thought that right there would be enough to turn him off.

Daniel said, "He is really dashing, Danielle. I'm not interested, mind you, because I've got this thing going with Jonas that I don't want to ruin, but Marv is hot."

"You're wearing pot goggles. He is not." But then I looked again and realized he was, and that my crush on Jacob had blinded me to the beauty that was right before me. I had wasted my lust on a lesser man!

Ms. Harrison made us stay until the last seconds of the evening. We had to become part of the cleanup crew, which was fine with Daniel because he wanted to talk to Marv nonstop. He moved beyond thinking he was handsome and said the guy was just really smart. By night's end, Daniel was thinking he should study psychology instead of music. Men! (Although, Daniel would make a great therapist.)

At the end of the night, Marv gave me the biggest hug ever. It was nice. I was able to thank him with words out of my mouth and not on the page. I guess I'm evolving.

When we were finally allowed to leave, Daniel and I went to Iggie and Jonas's house for a private after-prom thing instead of going to the Meadow Oaks party. Keira actually invited me to it, which was awesome, but I explained that Daniel and I had already made other plans. I had social options—wow.

When we got to Jonas's, Daniel grabbed his guitar out of the car and took me around to the detached garage in the back of the house where Iggie was folding paper and holding a harmonica and Jonas was eJamming. I didn't know what this was, but they explained it to me. Essentially, it is this online resource where you can play live music with random people all over the world. You don't see each other like iChat; you just hear each other talk, sing, and play.

Jonas was playing drums while this guy in Germany who barely spoke English played the keyboards. Daniel joined in on the guitar and somebody in Arizona added bass. Occasionally, Iggie would look up from his paper creations and play the harmonica. It was literally an eJam. It sounded awesome, this world joined in music through cyberspace. Jonas handed me a USB headset and told me I should sing. It was a blues jam at the moment, and they said I should try to make up some sad lyrics to add to the mix, and I jokingly said that I had no experience with pain, so it would be better if we could just copy the stylings of some teenage pop star.

Daniel said, "Ha-ha. Channel Janis Joplin and start wailin'."

I listened to them for a moment and closed my eyes. I got really calm and felt a stirring from this new music that was happening right now in different places on the planet, converging in this garage. And then, with my body swaying and my eyes still closed, I just started smiling and singing:

"He called me a cow."

Ba-ba-da, bum-bum.

"He *moo*'d in my face."

Ba-ba-da, bum-bum.

"Yes! He called me a cow!"

Ba-ba-da, bum-bum.

"I couldn't run any place.

'Cause I got the Mr. *Moo*-ooo-ooo-Me

Moo-You blues . . ."

And then all the different sounds exploded, and Iggie really rocked the harmonica. All the guys started singing the "Mr. *Moo* You Blues," even the guy in Germany, who added deep and lowing *moos*. This went on and morphed for at least forty-five minutes. At the end I felt sweaty and high, and I wasn't even stoned. German man asked Iggie, "Ver'd you get da sexy sounding frauline?"

Jonas said, "She's my boyfriend's fruit fly."

And the German guy said, "Oh, cool" like he understood, but we knew he didn't.

So, prom night was an evening of dressing up, dancing, getting stoned, singing, singing again, and then feeling stoned without any drugs at all. When it was nearly morning, Iggie walked me to the car so Jonas and Daniel could say good-bye privately. He made an elaborate, paper butterfly while we were all jammin', and he gave it to me before he turned around and ran into his house. I stared at it for a long time and moved it in figure-eight motions in the air, so I could watch the delicate wings go up and down.

When Daniel finally got into the car, he grabbed my hand and smiled at me. We shared a long joyous stare and then drove home in silence because nothing more needed to be said for the night. As we pulled into my driveway, another line of Emily Brontë's rose in my mind: "Whatever our souls are made of, his and mine are the same."

(A)

Danielle Carmen Levine

English 12

Ms. Linda Harrison

Period 4

I know we're supposed to wait until we graduate to call you by your first name, but I'm not really "calling you" Linda because I'm writing it. Hope that's permissible. It's a nice name. My middle name is Carmen, as you can see. It's weird to think this is the last essay I will write for a grade in English class for all of high school. I have to just take a moment and let that sink in. New paragraph.

After many discussions at my house with my aunt Joyce and my parents, I've decided to go to UC Irvine. I don't want to brag about myself in writing (although I think I've done that a couple of times this year), but I got a really high score on the verbal portion of the SATs (the math: not so much). The verbal score, I think, helped me get into colleges I probably wouldn't have gotten into. I'm going to UC Irvine as a creative writing major. As *serendipity* (I love this word, thanks for fitting a few last minute vocabulary words into my head; I think they'll come in handy) would have it, my friend Daniel got into UC

Irvine and is going there, too, but he's going undecided. My aunt said if we were sleeping together she would never let us attend the same college. But since that exchange is pretty much off the table because Daniel is gay, she saw it as all good.

Everybody is finding it very strange (even me) that I am going to go to college in the same area where, well, you know, a part of me stopped. You know from that one essay I read in class that a terrible thing happened to me in Orange County. I guess my mom had a talk about this situation with David, my yoga teacher, one day after class, and he told her that often you have to go back to a place of wounding to be fully healed. I don't quite understand that, but I do feel like something in me is guiding me there. For one thing, their creative writing department is very good, and maybe I will learn how to be a better writer and do all the things you wish I could already do with my writing. I'll e-mail you some stuff I write after I learn more (not that you didn't teach me enough, just that I guess I wasn't ready for all of it) and if you have time, you can tell me what you think.

So, I'm going to UC Irvine. I'm going to be an anteater. That's a good mascot for me. I'm not ready to be a tiger or a Titan or anything that fierce yet. I think I've grown a lot this year, but I'm still scared about some things, and I'm probably always going to be obsessive and inattentive, so I have to "take 'er easy," eat one ant at a time, if you will.

Comments from Ms. Harrison: *Since there were no formal guidelines given for this essay, I will not lecture you on all the* *parentheticals and casual comments contained therein. I will just remind you, once again, to avoid "a lot" and "stuff." Grow past that usage. Have a wonderful experience at UC Irvine. You deserve it.*

ME-MOIR JOURNAL 6/25
Graduation

Commencement finally came for me. I wanted to wear my blue Chucks that I had recently painted the word *abide* across, but my father said I didn't need those. He believed I was capable of going out in the world in heeled shoes, and, on my own, I could give over to the day and embrace the experience. After all, I had a hat—the graduation cap I would wear for this one day. I think I managed to handle things in a way that honored his wishes.

My parents dropped me off at the ceremony site early as was required for pictures and rehearsal. As I was walking in from the parking garage, Iggie appeared from out of nowhere. He threw an entire box of oragami art all over me. He didn't say a word. I stood there as an avalanche of snow creatures—giraffes, fishes, birds, dogs, and even some hummingbirds fell on me and around me as if I were the centerpiece in a living snow globe. For a moment, I became my own favorite collectible. After Iggie ran away, before I could even thank him for this most amazing gift, I collected every paper masterpiece—all two hundred of them, such a great even number. I will have to spend more time inspecting this menagerie, and I'll keep them forever.

Everyone in my class was delirious with excitement. Right before the ceremony began, we gathered in an annex that was part of the concert hall where our graduation took place. All of the students showered Ms. Harrison and Marv with gifts. They didn't open them there, but when they do, I hope Marv likes the giant red clown shoes I bought him, and I hope Ms. Harrison can appreciate the box of temporary tattooes I picked out especially for her.

Ms. Harrison gave us last-minute instructions, and we met the bagpiper who would soon usher us into our places. She warned us that there were hundreds of people in the room, all there for us and that we needed to be on our best behavior. She had to confiscate two beach balls and a bullhorn from some of the boys. Even though our graduating class was small, it was clear we were well loved.

"The room is packed," she said. "Stay in the moment. Try not to move around and crane your necks looking for your family and friends. Be formal as the day requires and your loved ones will find you afterward. I'm proud of all of you."

After the bagpiper led us in, there were some speeches from school board members that nearly put me to sleep. But then, there was a video that showed a year-in-review. It was great, and I got emotional but was able to swallow my rising tears. Next, there was a performance by our sign language class. A group of seniors signed a song and then awards were given out.

I drifted off again during that section because I didn't think I'd win anything. I was wrong. I won this year's Meadow Oaks Writing Award! It was very surprising to me because I seemed to rarely be able to follow all of Ms. Harrison's rules, and I thought that I frustrated her more than I made her happy. She must have liked what I wrote this year anyway.

Ms. Harrison handed me my plaque through genuine tears. I gave her a big hug, looked at her, and quietly said, "Thank you, Ms. Harrison. For everything. I will always remember you." When I walked back to sit down, I saw that my classmates had stood up for me and that Keira was whistling loudly. This was the first time I ever got an award for anything. It was totally cool.

After all our names were called, after "Pomp and Circum-stance," that was when a big surprise came. All the organized ceremony melted into group chaos. Kids were looking for their families, people were shouting and laughing and crying. Keira yelled over people's heads at me and said, "Hey, Danielle, your parents and other people are looking for you."

My group finally found me. They pushed their way through. Daniel practically knocked me over when he hugged me. He was so excited about my writing award, so glad they didn't give it to a quarterback, he said. When he let go of me, I saw around his shoulder: Aunt Joyce, Mom, Dad, and . . . Justine! I screamed. My aunt had flown her out as a graduation present to me, the best ever. There must have been some real dirty pool going on with my mail, but I am going to accept that because I was happy to see my beautiful, British friend. She was so excited to have "journeyed to California" and was looking forward to a few days with my family and Daniel—it was her first trip to the States. She was wearing a corsage, and I knew my father had bought it for her. I was glad he did.

Justine handed me a gift wrapped in heavy, coarse paper and tied with a string. She wove dried purple and blue flowers around the string; the whole thing was so lovely that I didn't want to open it, but she begged me to. She clapped her hands together and rose up on her toes as I started to unwrap her gift, and we all let out a little giggle at cute, kid-like, eighty-year-old Justine. She just couldn't wait until we got home for me to see my gift.

Before I got it fully opened, Justine said, "I want you to know that it's been years since I've tried to paint and write in calligraphy. Oh my, I used to do it ages ago when my fingers worked better. But I had an idea in my head what I wanted to see come out on a page, so I made my doctor come over to my flat and give me something that could help my fingers work for just a few hours. Oh, but miracles."

I told her that I was sorry she had to be in pain to make me a gift, that I didn't want that for her. She said she didn't tell me that story to make me feel sorry for her. In fact, she wasn't sorry at all. Her sore fingers made what she created all the more meaningful and rich and that after living a little longer, I would see that in pain there are wonderous buried treasures if you are brave enough to dig. I wanted to stop for a minute and take in all that she had said and talk to her about it, but everyone was yelling at me to get the thing opened, so I did.

In a small, ancient-looking frame was a watercolor painting of a chubby, redheaded ballerina in motion. One of her hands was lifted above her head with her fingers spread in that graceful way that good dancers can do. From that palm, a cascade of colorful flowers fell to a blue stream beneath her feet. They made the water look like a rainbow. In the dancer's other hand was an open scroll that had a Rumi poem written in perfect, tiny calligraphy. My family made me read the poem out loud to them, and even though there were hundreds of people in the concert hall, I only heard myself say:

You Are Not a Single You
> When you fall asleep,
> you go from the presence of yourself
> into your own true presence.
> You hear something
> and surmise that someone else in your dream
> has secretly informed you.
> You are not a single "you."
> No, you are the sky and the deep sea.
> Your mighty "Thou," which is nine hundredfold,
> Is the ocean, the drowning place
> Of a hundred "thous" within you.

Justine said she wanted to give me something I could take to college with me to hang on my wall that would remind me that

I am more expansive than I can ever imagine. Everyone loved the poem and the watercolor ballerina that Justine said was me as I dance through this life.

We all went back to my house for brunch and even Daniel's parents came. Our parents really got along well, and I thought that maybe Daniel's family and my family were all wired by the universe to somehow be compatible even though we were different in some ways. For example, Daniel's parents are so religious. That worked out in our favor, though, because Justine wanted to go to church tonight because she has never missed a Saturday night Mass since Bubbles died.

While all the other kids in my class were probably at graduation parties, I went to church. Justine said that was just fine because there are necessary rituals for all people at different times in their lives.

Daniel's family, my family, and Justine went to five o'clock Mass at Daniel's Catholic church. Nobody in my family acted uncomfortable or like they didn't belong there even though I knew we didn't. I didn't understand a lot of what went on, but I did like shaking hands with people to make a sign of peace. I thought that was a cool thing for a church to do. After the Mass, we did the thing that was so important to Justine, that was the reason she wanted to go to church tonight. We lit candles at the back of the church. Justine said I could make an offering and then light a candle and offer that light up to my God in any way I wanted to.

I watched Justine light her candle and close her eyes, and

after a few minutes a smile seemed to grow on her face from a great place inside her. I think she inspired everyone because all of us lit candles. Before Daniel went, he nudged me a little and glanced down at his crotch, proud to show me that he no longer gets boners in church. (Yoga teacher David would have been proud of Daniel for learning to "soften something." LOL.)

I went last. Everyone waited around me, and although no one knew what I was thinking, I felt their silent support hold me up. I actually lit three candles. The first one was for Emily, to thank her for being the best friend a young girl could have. The second was for the man who killed Emily, so I could learn how to see him in a compassionate light. And the third one was for me. To forgive myself for being alive.

After that, we all went bowling, which was something Justine wanted to watch us do while she drank a pint of ale.

Acknowledgments

OCD, *The Dude, and Me* reflects the work of a tribe of literary people to whom I am forever indebted. My agent, Amy Burkhardt, is an angel of the highest order. Thank you, Amy, for working diligently to make this story better, for being so patient and professional, for leading me through this process and for giving your time generously. You are a gift. Big thanks to Maria Dinzeo for her keen notes and for liking what she saw enough to pass it along. To Jen Hunt, my outrageously talented editor. Thank you for seeing what this story could be, for giving me such thoughtful, wise guidance and for being so encouraging. You are awe-inspiring. To both Amy and Jen, thank you for taking a chance on me. Another round of thanks goes to all the enthusiastic experts at Penguin for their work on this book, especially to Rosanne Lauer and Sarah Davis Creech for their artistry and to Megan Looney for her care.

To Dr. Robert Brooks and Rick Lavoie, the best of teacher and student advocates, whose work made me a better teacher. Their ideas influenced this story.

Huge heartfelt shout-outs to the beautiful peeps in my life who kept nudging me along and easing my anxiety through the writing process: Seth Donsky, Matt Kaminsky, and Carrie Robinson, you get your wings for reading this manuscript a crazy number of times and still remaining friends with me.

Thank you, Ken, "dumb guy" Weiler Weiner and all The Four Postmen.

Thank you, Bruce Seifert, for the "fruit fly" bit.

Thank you, Peter Murphy, for your time and expertise.

To my dear colleagues, the ones I ate lunch with, laughed with, cried with, and learned from: You change lives. To all my students, past and present, for enriching my life immeasurably. A special nod to the courageous class of 2012 and their families—bless you people. To the Seleca-Teshes, the Turners, and Lisa Maki for the extra love you gave me when I needed it the most.

To Carrie, Mina, Karen, Dotty, Charlotte, Kathy, Katharine, Dorothee, Liz, Jeri, Patty, Cynthia, Lainie, Wendy, Michelle, Laura, Mary Jane, Renee, Diane, Kim, the Krisses, the Loris, the Nancys, the Laurens, and the Moonbows—girlfriends who feed and nurture my soul. A writer must have soul food, and you gals provide the most delicious kind.

To all my yoga instructors, who keep me calm and remind me to breathe. A special thanks to Christie William and Daniel Stewart, who have been yoga preachers to me for years now.

To the Coen brothers, who have given me an obsession that continues to entertain and heal me.

To Parviz for Rumi.

To Mike Ozar and Mandana Chambers for their precious care of my dreams and my psyche.

To my family: the Roedersheimers, Vaughns, Thiels, and Hessees. I'm happy Life saw fit to bring us together. To all my nieces and nephews, the dearest of the dear. I hope I can support you with the same loving spirit demonstrated to me by all my amazing aunts. (My uncles are cool, too.) Thank you Mom, Dad, and Rob…for everything. And yes, Rob, you helped.